# Forever With You

## BAXTER BOYS
### BOOK THREE

## JESSIE GUSSMAN

# Contents

# Acknowledgments

**Cover art by Julia Gussman**
**Editing by Heather Hayden**
**Narration by Jay Dyess**
**Author Services by CE Author Assistant**

~

Listen to the unabridged audio for FREE performed by Jay Dyess on the Say with Jay channel on YouTube. Get early access to all of Jay's recordings and listen to Jessie's books before they're available to the general public, plus get daily Bible readings by Jay and bonus scenes by becoming a Say with Jay channel member.

# Chapter One

Tough clicked "publish" and allowed a small smile to hover on the corners of his lips. Funny how the words that never came easily out of his mouth flowed without effort from his fingers.

Placing his hands behind his head and leaning back with a loud squeak from the ancient, wobbling office chair, he allowed himself a grunt of satisfaction as his phone began chiming with notifications.

He had just reached to shut his computer screen off when a squeal and crash shook the walls of the old warehouse. His chair's legs slapped back down on the concrete. He jumped to his feet and strode out of the office, through the cavernous, cement-floor interior that he used as his garage. He passed the now-deserted checkerboard, where retirees sat during the day while he worked on customers' cars, and grabbed the knob of the side door. The warehouse wasn't exactly square, and the old metal door always required a good jerk to slip it out of its frame.

Tough yanked. The door flew open.

Just off the sidewalk in front of his building, an older model car with minimal front-end damage sat beside a light-colored hybrid. The damage to the hybrid was heavier but still not extensive. According to the placement of the cars, it looked like the older one cut the corner too close and clipped the hybrid as it sat at the stop sign.

Tough's heart did a light stumble as he recognized the perky little blond who had jumped out of her little hybrid and was walking around. Kelly Irwin. Her face scrunched up as though in pain when she saw the damage to her car. But she didn't stop, continuing to the driver's side of the other vehicle.

He glanced in the window of her car. Normally she had at least two underprivileged children with her anywhere she went outside of her job as a social worker supervisor. Not today.

Tough didn't see anyone else in the other car, either.

The older gentleman had gotten out, meeting Kelly over his door.

Kelly lifted a hand to keep long strands of honey blond hair out of her face as a breeze tunneled down between the two large buildings on either side of the street. "Are you okay?" She let go of her hair and touched the man's arm.

He rubbed his head. "I'm fine. I can't believe how much damage there is. I wasn't going that fast!"

She smiled reassuringly at him, her whole face lighting up, and patted his arm. "I know you weren't." She held her hand out. "I'm Kelly, by the way."

"Grant Hormell." The man shook her hand, but the worry lines never eased from his face.

Tough considered the damages and figured it was true; he really wasn't going very fast. It might look like a lot, but really, the damage was minimal. Easily fixed in his shop where he did body and motor work.

At this point, Tough knew, any "normal" person would have walked over with their hand out. They'd introduce themselves and mention the auto body shop they owned just behind them. They'd mention that their shop had just emptied out this morning. They'd offer to give an estimate, get the cars in, and have them fixed by closing tonight.

Tough clenched his jaw. His eye twitched. Unfortunately, his unusual name was the most normal thing about him. Always had been.

Kelly opened her mouth, but the man spoke again. "I'm so sorry. I dropped my phone, and I just leaned over to pick it up, and that's when..."

"Yes, it's okay," Kelly said gently. "I know these things happen so fast. Please don't feel bad. Nobody was hurt. That's the important thing. The cars can be fixed." She patted his arm.

The man twisted his hands together and took a shaky breath. "I hate to ask this of you, but could we keep from reporting this? My kids have been trying to take my license from me for a year now, and once I lose it..."

Kelly's hand stayed consolingly on the man's arm, and his hands quit twisting together. "Hey. It's okay. I understand. It could have happened to anyone. We don't have to report this."

"Really?" The man looked like he was going to hug Kelly. But then his face fell. "I won't be able to pay for your repairs up front. I'm on social security. But I can do payments."

"Let's take it one step at a time." Kelly shifted and looked at the front of the man's car. "I think your car will be fine." Her face tightened when she looked at her own. "Mine, not so much. I don't know how much that will cost." Kelly held up the phone in her hand. "I can Google body shops."

Tough leaned out toward the street and looked up at the admittedly battered homemade sign above his door. "*Tough Bodywork.*" He'd deliberately not put an apostrophe "s" on the end of his name. Enough people had ribbed him about the idiotic names his father had given him and his brothers before his dad split for good. He'd decided he might as well make a play on it himself when he named his shop.

The name wasn't the only thing he'd been made fun of for over the years. He'd learned a long time ago it was better to twist life to suit him than to wait for others to twist it to hurt him.

He straightened and looked back out on the street, at the cars that were less than ten feet from him. At the people who were not much farther away. How was he always invisible to flesh-and-blood humans? Why was it always so hard for him to get past the debilitating unease around strangers, especially women? Double that for Kelly.

If only he'd gotten even an ounce of his brother Turbo's ability to lead with a joke.

Tough cleared his throat.

The man shifted nervously. Kelly's fingers flew over her phone. The bright red nail polish glinted and flashed. The earrings dangling at her lobes clinked. The woman was never still and seldom quiet.

A tight little ball formed in the back of Tough's throat. He swallowed it away. It didn't bother him at all that most people didn't notice him. He actually preferred it that way. It did bother him some that Kelly seemed to be the same as most people, at least in that area.

"Oh, it says that there's one real close to here." Kelly's brows furrowed as she looked up, around, and behind her at the building across the street.

Tough crossed his arms over his chest and leaned against the wall. *Not there, Kelly.*

She looked back down at her phone and tilted her head, as though trying to figure out which way to read the map.

So he stood watching as Kelly made a slow turn, her white and blue dress puffing out in the breeze, looking up and down the dilapidated buildings at the end of the street.

Tough's heart pumped harder, faster as her gaze moved closer. She saw the sign first. She glanced at her phone then back to the sign. A smile tugged up the ends of her lips. His heart stumbled. Her gaze swept down the building. Her eyes widened as they landed on him.

His eye twitched, and the muscle in his jaw bunched. He didn't even try to swallow the lump in his throat. From past experience, he knew he'd never be able to speak around it anyway. He had always been tongue-tied with strangers, and women in particular. He came out of the womb that way. Unfortunately.

He could talk cars, so he'd never had a problem in his shop, until a customer started talking about the weather or the ball game or, God forbid, something more personal.

Sparkling white teeth flashed in Kelly's perfectly tanned face. Her dress swooshed around her legs as she hurried toward him, her hazel eyes bright and clear, polite enquiry on her face.

"Excuse me, sir. Could you tell me if the auto body shop behind you is open?"

"Yeah." Tough managed to get one word past the logjam in his throat.

Kelly paused, as though waiting for him to say more. When he didn't, her pink lips pursed, then she smiled even brighter.

"So, is it, or isn't it?" She spoke slower, the way many people did when they talked to him.

His chest burned a little.

"Yeah," he said again. That word and "no" were the two words he knew he could almost always get past his closed-up throat. They were sufficient in most situations.

"Okay, great. Then I'll just head inside and talk to the owner." She started to brush past him.

He forced his mouth open. "That's me."

She stopped so fast her sandals almost left skid marks on the sidewalk. Spinning around, her dress billowed out, brushing his jeans, reminding him of his airbrush with its light touch and attention to detail. Only it made his leg hot, like a welding burn. Her perfume flirted with his nose. He breathed deep to catch its full-bodied flavor. It was the smell of money with sunshine and glitter. Her hair shimmered like wet paint in the sun.

Her eyes met his, but he couldn't stand the intimacy, and his gaze skidded over her shoulder to the peeling metal behind her.

"I'm sorry, Mr.—" She looked down at her phone. "—Baxter." Her head snapped up. "Hey, you're Torque's brother."

Tough jerked his head up in agreement. Yep. He was Torque's brother.

"I didn't know your shop was here."

"It is." He cursed his stupid tongue that knotted every time he tried to use it.

"Well, that's just great." She held her hand out. "I'm Kelly."

He knew her.

"My best friend, Cassidy, is marrying your brother."

Knew that too.

He held his dirty hands up to show her he wasn't being rude by not shaking her outstretched hand.

She grabbed his hand as he raised it and pumped it anyway. "I've heard so much about you," she said, her smile bigger and brighter up close. "I think we've been that close," she held up two fingers about an inch apart, "to meeting several times over the last six months since Torque got out of prison..." Her voice trailed off like she was afraid she'd offended him by mentioning his brother's prison record.

She needn't worry. His brother was a fine man, and Tough was not ashamed.

Kelly's fingers felt slender and cool as they disappeared in his rough grasp. His throat tightened even more. He looked away so she wouldn't see the tic of his eye.

"Well, um, would you have time, and would you be able to give me an estimate on fixing my car?" She gave a little laugh. "And check Mr. Hormell's car, too?"

Tough jerked his head up. "No." His gaze skidded across her, avoiding her startled look, and focused on the damage. He'd seen Kelly around. A lot. That bright yellow car was hard to miss. No one else around here drove a hybrid, either. Especially not a Cadillac hybrid. He'd heard, from the rumor mill, that the car was a gift from her fiancé.

Tough didn't know how that fiancé thing played out, exactly. But he knew what she did with her spare time, the kids she helped, and the money she spent on her own to ease the struggle of poor children in this town. She wasn't paying him a dime for this.

He was saving to rent the other half of the warehouse so he could expand his shop, but he would do that without Kelly's money. She hadn't been born rich, although she was engaged to marry money.

"Oh." The smile slipped a little from her face before she fastened it back on, brighter. "Well, could you give me a recommendation for another shop?"

A car ambled down the street, the driver rubbernecking at the two banged-up autos as it passed by.

Tough watched the brake lights come on as the car stopped at the stop sign at the intersection. She had misunderstood him. Somehow, he had to find the words to correct her, then get them out of his mouth, or she was going to walk away from him.

"I can do it." It sounded more like a growl than actual speech to his ears, but at least the words were out.

The older gentleman walked closer and stood with his arms crossed.

"He looks like he can handle it, but is this a reputable company? I'd hate it if you got fleeced on top of what I've done."

Before Tough could react, Kelly stepped between the man and him. Her finger waved in the air, and her little sandal, with its skinny, pointy heel, stomped on the sidewalk. He could almost feel the head of steam building up inside of her. The side of his mouth tugged up. Slowly, like it was rusty.

"Tough Baxter has a reputation around town for excellence in body work. I didn't realize this was his shop at first, but I've heard only good things about him. His brother is a prodigy with motors. The whole Baxter family has the kind of intelligence that enables them to fix anything." She punctuated her words with her waving finger.

There was nothing slow about the movement of Tough's mouth this time. After he pulled his chin off the ground, both sides were smiling at her offhand compliment. How could she know that about him?

"Oh, I'm sorry. I didn't know." The man stepped back. "I really need my car. I know I'm not in a position to make demands, but can he have it done quickly? Maybe by tomorrow?"

Kelly said, "That's asking a little much, I think."

"It'll be done," Tough ground out.

Kelly whipped around. "Seriously?" she hissed in a softly shouted whisper.

Tough didn't move. He couldn't. He'd never been this close to her before, although he'd seen her plenty of times from far away. Color infused her cheeks. Her lively eyes seemed to sparkle and snap. He could almost feel the tingling energy that surged off her. Tempted to touch her, just to see if she would shock him like an electric fence, he resisted, keeping his arms folded over his chest.

He nodded slowly.

She tilted her chin, acknowledging his nod, then looked back at the older gentleman. "That's good with you?"

Reading people wasn't his strength. Heck, there wasn't much that was his strength. But he could fix cars. Or trucks. Or busses, bikes, boats. Heck, he could probably even do body work on a locomotive, not that he'd ever had the opportunity to try. So Tough wasn't sure what, exactly, Mr. Hormell was thinking as he huffed out a breath and took another look at his older model car.

"How much?" the man asked, rubbing his chin. "And when?"

Tough didn't have to calculate. The cost, time, and complexity of the repair had automatically computed in his head when he'd first seen the accident. He couldn't tell about Kelly's car, just because he couldn't tell from this distance whether or not the headlight holder had cracked or whether any pieces of the grill had punctured any part of the front end of the motor. Both of those things were common. And both would complicate repairs. He could do it. It would just take longer. He still wasn't charging.

"By midnight," he said. After he fixed the dent, he'd have to spray primer and give it time to set before spraying the color-matched paint and then the clear coat. He gave an estimate on the price, grateful now that the shop had emptied out that morning.

The man nodded. "Fine." He held out his hand. "Mr. Hormell."

Tough nodded and shook his hand.

"Thank you, Mr. Baxter." Kelly bounced to the cars. "I can take you home, Mr. Hormell."

"No," Tough said. Hearing Kelly call him Mr. Baxter didn't sit right. But there was no way he was going to find the words to tell her about that.

She put a hand on her hip, planted her tiny sandals on the pavement, and opened her mouth.

Tough didn't let her start. He forced his mouth open. "Don't drive it 'til I check it."

Took the wind right out of her sails. Her whole body deflated like a flat tire in summer. "Oh," she said meekly. She looked over at her car. "I guess something might be wrong with the motor or something..."

Yeah. And the Pope would ice skate in hell before Tough allowed her to drive away alone with a stranger.

He glanced toward Mr. Hormell. "I'll get them off." He nodded at the wrecked cars. "Then I'll take you."

Mr. Hormell shifted. "I'm from Scranton and was staying in a hotel for the night."

Tough nodded.

He stopped in the act of turning away when cool fingers landed on his arm. A light touch, but a vice couldn't have stopped him faster. As much as he wanted, really wanted, to look down and meet her eyes, he just couldn't force himself to be that intimate. He set his jaw, angled his head so his ticking eye pointed away from her, fastened his eyes at a point over her left shoulder, and waited.

"Could you...would you mind taking me to the community center across town?"

She volunteered there after she put in a full day as a social worker supervisor. It's where she got most of the kids she was always dragging around, picking them up and dropping them off at their houses. But a part of him didn't want her to know that he knew so much about her.

Experience had taught him that most people used their mouths more than their eyes and ears and they expected the rest of the world to do the same. That same experience said that she would be freaked out, think he was a stalker, weird, or worse, if she knew the facts he knew about her life and habits. Just from watching and listening. He breathed deeply through his nose. And now he had a scent to attach to all of that information. His arm burned. A scent, and a cool touch that scalded his skin.

He forced his eyes to meet hers for a fraction of a second before they skipped away.

"The community activity center on 15th Street," she said slowly.

He was able to get his gaze to land on her dress but couldn't quite meet her eyes. His eyebrow twitched.

"I volunteer there," she added.

"Yeah," he ground out, trying not to look like he knew. He wanted to tell her to wait, that he'd get the cars off the street and come back for her, but his back was turned and his feet were walking away, and his tongue never did unknot itself.

# Chapter Two

Broad shoulders and narrow hips moved away from Kelly without a word of explanation. Should she follow him? She felt like an idiot just standing here. Being inactive, letting other people take charge, those weren't exactly traits that came naturally to her. But Torque's brother had left her with little choice. Torque, Tough...what odd names their family had. She had a vague recollection of hearing it before... somewhere. A memory teased at the back of her mind, but she couldn't catch the strand and pull it up.

She'd known Torque had a brother—she'd heard more than once from Cassidy what a mechanical whiz he was—but she hadn't known he was so...rugged. Quiet. Gruff. And obviously didn't want to be bothered by her.

Checking her messages again, although her phone hadn't buzzed or dinged, she sighed. No one had answered her. Cassidy was working. The ladies at the center were busy with kids. Her fiancé, Preston— how odd to finally think of him as her fiancé after practically growing up together—was probably busy, even though this was his day off. She glanced down at the new, very large ring on her left hand. She had never said "yes" when he asked. He slipped the ring on like he'd known she was expecting it. Everyone expected them to get married, and she really did love him. Just a quiet love; no sparks or bells or whistles.

And his mother, Mrs. Fitzsimmons, had done so much for Kelly. She was more of a mother than her own mother had been. How could she not marry Preston? Mrs. Fitzsimmons had been over the moon when Preston had finally announced their engagement. Everyone had been expecting them to get married, probably since high school.

She gave the ring a last look. It was pretty.

Marrying Preston would make Mrs. Fitzsimmons happy, but it didn't solve Kelly's problems. Like the fact that the community activity center had a roof that leaked, and the landlord kept promising to fix it but refused to take the money and do so. Plus, it was across town, too far for most kids to walk, and she ended up driving around the city, picking them up and dropping them off every day. It was worth it to keep them off the streets, but it sure would be nice to find a suitable building in the area and open a new center. One that didn't leak every time it rained. Unfortunately, the red-hot economy had the unanticipated consequence of snatching up available real estate.

Taking one last glance at her phone, she shoved it in her purse.

She looked back at her banged-up Cadillac hybrid. The kids in these neighborhoods needed her. She was making a difference in their lives, just as Mrs. Fitzsimmons had made a difference in hers. That was the most important thing to her. And if she had a few misgivings about the lukewarm attraction between her and Preston? She would shove them aside. Preston and she made a perfect match. Mrs. Fitzsimmons was happy, and Kelly could keep working with the neglected and needy children in this town. That was really all that mattered.

Kelly hurried over to Mr. Hormell and offered her arm as he attempted to shuffle up the curb.

"Thank you, miss," he said.

She glanced over as Tough bent and lifted the garage door, the muscles in his back and arms bunching and stretching his tee. She clasped her hands together, trying not to remember the rough feel of his calloused hand closing around hers. It should have felt claustrophobic, as big and strong as it was. But it hadn't. It had felt warm and solid and right. A feeling that had surprised her.

Too bad the man couldn't seem to force himself to talk to her.

Tough climbed into Mr. Hormell's car and drove it slowly off the street and into his garage.

She smiled at Mr. Hormell and struck up a conversation about the weather, while wondering what it was about Tough that made her eyes want to follow his every move. It wasn't his charming personality; that was for sure. And there was something about him, something that nagged in the back of her head, like she'd known him before.

She forced herself to pay attention to Mr. Hormell as Tough strode back out and lifted the hood on her car. Had she ever seen a man with such a confident walk? His whole posture was loose and relaxed. Casual.

She was never loose or relaxed, and she certainly didn't do casual.

Excusing herself from Mr. Hormell, she stepped quickly over to Tough and stuck her head under the hood. Maybe it was just an excuse to be near him, since she'd never actually seen anything that was under the hood of any car that she'd ever driven. Just like Preston had never seen her without her makeup armor.

"How bad is the damage?" Would she need to rent a car?

Tough pointed to the area around the headlight. "Cracked."

Kelly nodded, although she had no idea what that meant. "That's bad?"

"Expensive." He shifted, and a whiff of his manly scent drifted to her nose. Not expensive cologne or aftershave. Nothing like the way Preston smelled. But a mixture of grease and oil and gasoline underlaid with a straight-up male potency. Were there male pheromones? Kelly tried to remember from the one science class she'd taken in college. What else could explain this odd pull that had her breathing deeply and stepping closer?

"Will it take long to fix it?" Her voice held a freak husky note. She swallowed to try to get rid of it.

"Order parts." Tough lifted his head, but again, his eyes looked past her before he ducked back down and shifted away. Why wouldn't he look at her?

What did "order parts" mean anyway? Maybe some kind of mechanic slang. She wasn't going to pretend she understood. "You can fix it, but you don't have the parts?"

"Yeah." He didn't look up that time but kept his gaze on his hands which disappeared under some long, flat, black thingy. He manipulated a plastic lever, and something rattled, deep and low.

"That didn't sound good."

Tough shook his head. After checking several other places, he straightened and pulled a blue rag out of his pocket, wiping his hands. Kelly found herself fascinated with his short, black nails and long, agile fingers.

"Better tow it," he said.

"Can you fix it? Should I tow it somewhere that specializes in hybrids? Or Cadillacs?"

His hands stilled. She got the feeling he was using great effort. Maybe to keep from getting offended that she suggested someone else fix it?

"I can. Your choice." His words were short. Staccato, even. He shoved the rag into his back pocket. His eyes stared over her shoulder like he didn't give a flip what she chose.

She glanced at her phone, as if Preston would have magically texted her the answer. As if he'd even care where she got his car fixed.

She adjusted her purse strap over her shoulder and looked up. Tough's gaze landed on hers for a moment. Dark brown, swirled and layered like an expensive walnut floor. The zap from that brief eye contact ripped down her backbone and ricocheted back from her fingers and toes. She blinked. In that short flash, his gaze was gone, once again pinning something over her shoulder. His face, all sharp angles, except for the bump on his nose—evidence it was once broken—angled away from her.

"If you can fix it, I want you." That rogue husky note had crept back into her voice. To her ears, it sounded sultry, like she was on the other end of a 900 number. Which was ridiculous. She was a doer, a worker, as befitted the wife-to-be of a lawyer and aspiring politician. But not sultry. Not seductive. And definitely not sexy. She couldn't spend hours every day in front of a mirror getting her hair and makeup just right when there were children who needed her.

Tough stood with his hand on the hood of her car, waiting for her to step back so he could close it. Without giving him another glance, she hurried over to Mr. Hormell.

"He's going to get my car off the street, then he'll take us to your hotel."

Tough hadn't said any such thing. But Kelly wasn't going to wait around while he got over whatever chip he had on his shoulder and managed to tell her what he was doing. She'd make it up, first.

Mr. Hormell pulled a handkerchief out of his pocket and wiped at the sweat that rolled down his forehead. After seeing his flushed face, Kelly took his arm. "How about we move over there to the shady side of the building?" she suggested.

He nodded and allowed her to lead him around where the temperature was noticeably cooler. Kelly willed Tough to hurry. Not because she was in a rush, which she was, she always was, but because Mr. Hormell needed to be back in the air conditioning. Despite being late May, the central Pennsylvania humidity made the actual air temperature feel like the south side of hell.

A rumbling caused her to turn her head back toward where they had been standing. Tough's tow truck, which looked to be older than Kelly, puffed black smoke and rumbled as he backed it slowly toward the front of her car. Tough hopped easily from the cab, his limbs sure and strong. His ball cap shaded those dark, walnut eyes, but Kelly stared anyway. For the first time, she saw in him a glimpse of the little boy he might have been. A boy like one of the many she worked with every day. He'd have been adorable.

Again, that feeling like she knew him, or should know him, hit her. Had she known him when they were younger? Back before Mrs. Fitzsimmons took her in? That seemed right, but she still couldn't remember. She squinted, studying his angled chin. He definitely had a strong profile. Quite handsome.

He glanced up, and she whirled away, guilty. There was no law against looking at someone, but now, from the way she jerked around, he'd have to know she'd been staring. Wonderful. And why? No reason other than those stupid pheromones. She remembered reading about them but didn't remember the antidote. Onions, probably.

Her eyes bounced then settled on the door on the far side of the building. Was that a "For Rent" sign? She checked Mr. Hormell, whose color had improved. "I'll be right back."

She hurried down the sidewalk to the door. Yep. For Rent. She punched the number from the sign into her phone and hit the green button. With her phone to her ear, she peered in the dirty glass.

A counter, a couple of broken stools, and a few partitions, some with holes that looked like they'd been punched.

Still. This location was perfect. So much closer to where all the kids lived. As long as the roof didn't leak, it would be perfect in every way. In fact, she glanced at her phone—not quite time for school to let out—some of the kids probably hung out on this very street. She picked up four girls and a little boy just two blocks over every day in the summer and took them to the children's center across town.

She tried the doorknob as the phone went to voice mail, not expecting it to open. It didn't twist—it was locked—but the latch hadn't caught, and the little bit of pressure she exerted had the door swinging in like the building wasn't quite square.

Her surprise had her hesitating as she started her message. "Um, hi. I'm Kelly Irwin. I'm interested in the building you have for rent on..." She looked back at the road sign, unsure what street she was on. Finding the street name, she read it off then rattled on, leaving her number.

After pushing the red "end" button, she stepped into the warm, dark interior, not really intending to trespass but hoping to see if the building would suit her purposes.

The placed smelled musty and slightly tangy, like someone had left their dirty, wet socks lying around. Dust particles floated thickly in the light that angled steeply in from the side window. Kelly walked farther back, noticing the stools, the pages of designs, an old needle. The last renter had maybe been a tattoo parlor. She moved back, around the partitions. Whatever equipment they used to administer a tattoo had been removed. Just papers, trash, and some broken pieces of plastic and other junk littered the floor.

She squinted at the ceiling. No drooping insulation or crumbling drywall. She glanced around. No wet patches on the floor.

She walked farther in. She could go right to negotiations about the price and length of lease if she already knew it would work.

With the partitions removed, there might be enough room for a basketball court. Sports were always good to keep kids involved and interested. But it couldn't be everything to a child.

She bit her lip as an old memory shimmered through her mind. It had been forever since she'd thought of her real parents. She never knew her dad. Her mother hadn't been interested. How Kelly survived as a baby and toddler, she'd never know, since she couldn't remember her real mother ever caring whether she was home or fed or clean or anything. Memories of being alone and scared, of having no one who cared and no place to go, were what drove her now.

Thankfully, back then, someone had wanted a little girl.

The image wavered in her mind. Her heart stumbled, and she stopped short in the dim interior.

Now she remembered where she knew Tough from. Of course. How could she have forgotten? He was the little boy who had taken her by the hand and led her little five-year-old self to Mrs. Fitzsimmons, Preston's mom. He didn't talk back then, either. She wasn't sure she even knew his name back then. And she hadn't seen him much after that.

Shaking her head, she walked deeper into the dark interior. Tough didn't seem to remember her. But she would always owe him for what he'd done. After all, if it hadn't been for Tough and Mrs. Fitzsimmons, who knows where she would have ended up with her dad completely gone and her mom drunk and high most of the time. Whatever the scenario, her mom didn't have time for Kelly. It was hard and hurtful as a child, but it made it a lot easier to relate to the kids she worked with now.

The darkness had gotten thick, so she fumbled with her phone to get the flashlight app up. Once the bright light cut through the darkness, she could see there was nothing much different in back. A door with a sign that indicated there was a restroom. She didn't even want to go there.

Another door. Curious if the space was wider than the open waiting and reception area, she tried this door. Unlocked but stuck. She shoved. It moved enough to encourage her to gear up for a harder, quicker shove. Leaning her shoulder into it and planting her feet, she bent her knees and rammed it hard.

The door stuck for a second then burst open in a shock of light and potent male air. She'd been expecting the burst and was prepared. However, the pointy heel of her sandal had not, apparently, been designed to be as sturdy as a B&E attempt required. It twisted and snapped, sending Kelly reeling, off-balance, headfirst into a well-lit office and stumbling into the steel-like rigidity of Tough Baxter's arms and chest.

# Chapter Three

Tough dropped his tow truck keys. They landed on the cement floor with a clang and rattle he barely heard.

Soft, fragrant hair blew across his face, wrapping around his neck like a silken whisper. The more substantial weight of Kelly hit his chest. Her hands gripped his shoulders. His arms automatically caught her as her dress billowed around his legs. He fumbled through reams of material and flailing arms to the soft, curvy woman under it all. His hands gripped her waist. He froze, legs braced, teeth gritted.

Maybe she felt his stillness. Or maybe she knew he wouldn't let her fall. Whatever it was, her thrashing ceased and her body became motionless, her face against his chest, one of her knees between his, and one bare foot stepping on his square-toed work boot. Her shiny, pink-painted toes were directly in his line of sight.

His stomach clenched, and his insides quaked. His arms wanted to pull her closer. His nose wanted to bury itself in her sunshine and glitter scent. Never in his life had he wished harder that he had words. That he could use them to woo and win the packaged bundle of energy and empathy in his arms.

But this second, these few seconds, were an anomaly in his life.

Something to savor now and look back on with fond nostalgia and longing.

He did not allow his hands to move nor his head to shift. He did inhale, deeply, closing his eyes against the heat and happiness that made every muscle in his body strain to move.

Kelly shifted. A nervous laugh drifted out from under the hair that covered her face. One hand lifted from his shoulder and pushed long strands of hair out of her face.

Tough's insides twisted and cramped. Now he'd have to talk. Somehow. He'd like to ask her what she was doing. Why was she on the other side of the warehouse, wandering around? Unless...

His eyes shot to his computer. The screen saver—a truck being painted in time lapse—was still showing. Surely...surely she wasn't with the press? He knew her, knew her job, knew what she did...at least he thought he did. He'd been wrong before. Plus, he should know that sometimes people weren't what they seemed. He was the poster child for that.

She moved, and he dropped his hands from her waist. His fingers curved in, missing the sweet heat.

Maybe it was his imagination, but the hand still on his shoulder seemed to slide down his arm and give a tiny squeeze on his bicep before dropping off. His entire chest and arm felt like an overheated engine. It would not surprise him to see steam coming off any part of his body, but the parts that she had touched seemed especially combustive.

The weight on his foot disappeared. She bent and picked up the shoe that she had lost. He shifted so he stood in front of his computer screen, just in case that earlier, small suspicion proved correct. He crossed his arms over his chest, hoping her scent lingered in his office indefinitely. It was more than a little unbelievable there was any woman in his office, let alone Kelly. The farthest he'd ever thought was he might someday say hi to her. Today he'd touched her, memorized her scent, and if his stupid tongue would cooperate, he might even have a conversation with her. But it hung in his mouth, completely unconnected to his brain, while slow seconds ticked by.

"I'm awfully sorry about that," Kelly said after an uncharacteristic silence. She didn't look at him. Instead, she examined the sandal in her hand. The little, spiky heel hung at a crazy angle. "I suppose you're wondering what I was doing."

A little. More of his brainpower had been spent on wondering how to keep her in his office, how to have an actual conversation with her. And mostly wondering if she actually caressed his shoulder and bicep or if that were just his imagination. Why else would it be burning?

Kelly reached over and slapped her sandal against his desk. The faulty heel snapped off. The screen saver on his computer disappeared.

"Tough?" His landlord, Mr. Millard, walked into the office.

Tough jerked his head in greeting.

"I got your message...oh." He looked at Kelly. "I'm sorry." His confused gaze widened as he took in Kelly's bare feet. His cheeks reddened. Tough glanced down, and his own face heated. The long, flowing material of Kelly's dress had somehow gotten caught, and one long, tanned leg was completely exposed up to mid-thigh. Nothing more than he might see if she were wearing shorts, but it sure gave the appearance that something had been happening. Which was pretty obviously what Mr. Millard thought.

Mr. Millard wiggled his brows as his gaze went back to Tough. Tough shook his head, but Mr. Millard ignored him and grinned. "Don't usually see people in Tough's office." He held his hand out to Kelly. "I'm Jack Millard, Tough's landlord."

Kelly's bracelets clanked together as she stretched out her hand and shook his. Apparently, she'd been so focused on getting her shoe fixed that she hadn't noticed her dress situation. Tough considered himself pretty good at fixing stuff, but he had no idea how to fix this. Grab her dress and yank it? Telling her about it was completely out of the question. He wouldn't be able to get the word "leg" out of his mouth. He could point. But that might embarrass her.

"I'm Kelly Irwin. I think I may have just left you a message." Kelly finished shaking Mr. Millard's hand and braced herself on Tough's desk, lifting her foot and slipping her sandal back on. Her gaze hooked on his computer. There wasn't enough room for Tough to slip between her and his desk, so he did the only thing he could think of. He reached over and snapped the monitor off. It wasn't inconspicuous, but it got rid of the evidence. For now.

Kelly's eyes flicked to his. They narrowed. Tough didn't even bother to angle his face to hide the tic that fluttered his left eye. If she figured out the connection between him and what was on his computer screen, the gig was up.

Mr. Millard looked up from his phone. "This is your number?" He read it off.

Kelly nodded.

Mr. Millard glanced between Tough and Kelly. He seemed to sense that something wasn't quite right. Or that there was more going on. His gaze touched on Kelly's exposed leg before moving to Tough then back to Kelly. "I'd love to see Tough get a good neighbor, and you seem like a nice girl. The other side is yours if you want it." He quoted the amount needed, and Kelly nodded easily.

Tough's mouth opened. Kelly wanted to rent the other side? That was his. His jaw clenched. He'd been saving for the first and last months' rent, plus the deposit and the money it would take to remodel. He almost had it. Another week. He'd just texted that to Mr. Millard this morning. Forcing himself to relax—the place would be going to a good cause—he forced his teeth to quit grinding together.

Mr. Millard grinned and winked at Kelly. "I think your boyfriend here wanted to surprise you with it."

"No," Tough ground out.

"He's not my boyfriend," Kelly said at the same time. "I'm engaged." She held up her ring finger where a rock the size of a 6NZ motor caught the fluorescent lights and glowed yellowish.

Mr. Millard dropped his gaze to her leg and stared. "Maybe you let the wrong guy put that piece of gravel on your hand."

Kelly's gaze followed his. She gasped and swatted at her dress until it fell back into place where it belonged. "That was not...I..." She seemed to realize that she couldn't say exactly what happened, because after all, she had been technically trespassing on Mr. Millard's property.

Tough wanted to say he hadn't touched her, but that was technically not true, either. He hadn't lifted her dress up. At least not on purpose, if it had been something he did. He couldn't remember, didn't think it was him, but there had been a lot of flying limbs and material and hair and everything smelled so good, he couldn't really say for sure, even if he could get his mouth to work, which was doubtful.

Mr. Millard held his hands up. "Whatever. I'm not here to judge, and as long as I get my rent check, I don't care what hanky-panky you two are up to, although not many people surprise me, but Tough just did." The shrewd look he sent Tough's way made Tough want to step in front of his computer, even though he'd already switched the screen off. There was no way he could give Kelly everything she deserved, and he'd never ask her to be with him otherwise. But that didn't mean there wasn't something else he was hiding. He locked his knees to keep his foot from digging a toe in the cement floor.

Mr. Millard continued, "Obviously with a ring that size, the other guy's got money. I don't care, but Tough's a solid guy. He might not have the cash, but at least he'll never nag or insult you." Mr. Millard laughed at his joke.

Tough didn't look to see how Kelly took Mr. Millard's "humor." Wasn't the first time other people had laughed at his struggle or made jokes about it. Normally he didn't care, but he did kind of want to look good to Kelly, since she looked so good to him, even if he wasn't in contention for the position of being her man. Still, the small planet on her hand was a good reminder. It didn't really matter what she thought of him; she'd made a promise with another guy. Tough was old-school about promises.

Mr. Hormell hobbled into sight in the doorway. Talk about promises. He needed to get that man's car done by midnight. And he needed to take him to a hotel and get Kelly to the center before he could start. There wasn't time for him to stand around in his office, wishing the woman in it was his.

He'd come in here to begin with for his keys. He remembered dropping them. Searching the floor, he saw them lying between Kelly's feet. Figures.

Great. He couldn't pick them up. After all, he'd need to say "excuse me," and on a normal day, he might be able to get that out, but today was anything but normal. Then a rogue thought brought him up short. Why not? After all, she'd caressed his shoulder and bicep. He was sure of it. He could pick his keys up from between her feet.

He'd had a crummy childhood, yes. His dad had stuck around long enough to make four kids, saddle them with ridiculous names they were sure to be teased about for the rest of their lives, then he'd split, never to be heard from again. His mom had died of cancer not long after he'd started elementary school, and he and his brothers had gone to live with his gram, subsiding on social security and lots of home-canned food.

Still, he'd made one promise to his mother before she died—that he wouldn't be a womanizer like his dad—and he had every single intention in the world of keeping that promise. He'd walked the line. More than walked the line, he'd avoided even *looking* at the line from that time on. But today, for some reason, the devil was on his shoulder, and he couldn't shake him. So, ignoring the other people in the room, he turned his back to them and bent down to pick up his keys, trailing a finger over the soft skin and delicately sculpted bones of Kelly's ankle for one second before he stood back up.

# Chapter Four

Kelly stroked the curly head of the young girl who had just wrapped her arms around Kelly's waist and started to cry. Normally Jasmine was a precocious and sweet nine-year-old. But today she'd been sullen and depressed. Kelly had watched her for the past couple of hours, then, when Harris Winsted, the librarian in town and frequent volunteer at the children's center, had come in to read to the younger children, Kelly had taken Jasmine aside.

A few questions later, Jasmine's eyes had filled and she'd thrown her arms around Kelly, holding on like Kelly was the only solid thing in her world. Which, really, she was. Since Jasmine had just admitted that her parents were splitting.

"It's okay to cry, sweetie." Kelly's heart felt like it was shedding big, painful tears, too. Jasmine had such a beautiful smile and a generous heart.

"Mommy said Daddy isn't ever coming back." Jasmine sniffed into Kelly's shirt. "She said she hates him. And I said Daddy was good, and she said I was stupid to believe that." She started crying again and buried her head against Kelly's stomach.

Kelly squeezed Jasmine tighter, although what she really wanted to do was march over to Jasmine's house, grab her mother by the hair, and tell her never to bad-mouth Jasmine's father again.

She didn't say anything but held Jasmine against her and let her cry. This was a problem, all too common, that she couldn't fix. No amount of money could fix it, either. No government program. No breakfast program. No after-school program. Ugh.

Kelly stroked down Jasmine's back while the little girl sobbed. Several of the older children, sitting at the round tables in the far corner, had gone through this very thing. Her gaze was drawn back to the younger children sitting haphazardly around Harris on the large rug beside the tables, listening to her read. Many of those children didn't even have two parents at home. Of the ones who did, in Kelly's experience, over half would be in Jasmine's position someday.

She hadn't seen Jasmine's parents get married, but she'd bet they were smiling and happy and sharing their love with the world on that day. Half of all marriages ended in divorce. Yet, who ever heard of weddings where the bride and groom weren't smiling and "in love"? But all that "love" didn't keep their marriage together five or ten years later.

Jasmine's sobs had turned into an occasional hiccup. In Kelly's experience, and according to all the research she read, what just happened to Jasmine today would make her much more likely to hang out with the wrong friends. To drink alcohol. To do drugs. To drop out of school. To get pregnant as a teen. To have an abortion. To not go to college.

All because "love" wasn't enough to hold her parents together.

The big diamond ring on her hand felt heavy. Cold. What about her impending marriage? At least Preston and she would have a marriage build on friendship and mutual respect. They knew they'd make a good match —he wanted to be a politician and she would be the perfect politician's wife, while leaving plenty of time for her to focus on her charities, too.

But would that be enough? Did she love him enough? He said he loved her. She felt comfortable with him, even if there weren't any sparks. He felt comfortable enough with her that he'd finish her sentences. Or even assume her answer. So, when he'd held the ring up and she'd gasped and said, "What an amazing ring!", he'd grinned and slipped it on her hand, like that was a yes and her whole insides weren't clenching in total panic.

Kelly pulled a tissue out of her purse and helped Jasmine wipe her eyes. "I can't fix it, Jasmine. But I will always be here for you."

Jasmine nodded. After a few minutes, she wandered away, going over to the study tables and sitting down with her older sister. Kelly's heart broke a little more as her sister put an arm around her and pulled her close.

Gathering her things, Kelly walked over to the front door where they had a little kitchenette set up with a bar and stools along with a table and mismatched chairs. An old, yellow refrigerator was stocked with juice boxes and bottles of water. It was loud, but it kept things cold, so they put up with the noise.

Cassidy, her friend who was marrying Tough's brother, wore an apron over her power suit—she was a lawyer by day. As Kelly approached, Cassidy leaned over and took a tray of cookies out of the oven.

"I found a new place for us to rent." Kelly threw her purse on the counter and swiped a chocolate chip cookie baked in the shape of a dog's head from the cooling rack beside the sink.

"Do you ever stop?" Cassidy asked. She untied the apron from around her waist and glanced at the group of kids sitting in a circle on the floor still listening to Harris reading a book.

"Can't stop. There is so much that needs to be done and only a few people willing and able to do it." Kelly took a bite of the cookie, glancing at Jasmine and her sister before she grabbed a stack of books that needed to be sorted and organized.

"Well, you are still planning on stopping, at least for an evening and the next afternoon, for my wedding. Right?" Cassidy tilted her head, her no-nonsense bun highlighting the sharp angles of her face.

A little shot of nervous excitement, like the feeling of cresting the highest hill of a rollercoaster, snapped through Kelly. Tough would be at the wedding too. Probably as a groomsman. "Of course."

"Are you sure Preston isn't going to make it?"

"I'm sure." Kelly paused with a book in her hand. "He could never say no to being part of the delegation to Germany. This could be a defining moment in his career."

Cassidy set the folded apron down. "He would hate it anyway. He won't know anyone who's going to be there, but I want you to have a good time."

"I will." Kelly smiled at her friend, shoving her earlier thoughts about the lasting power of love aside. After all, Torque and Cassidy were not exactly conventional. From the adoption of the children, to the casual wedding that had been planned in six weeks. It certainly wasn't the big bash that Cassidy could afford.

Cassidy whistled as she scooped the last of the cookies off the tray. Kelly tilted her head. "I've never seen you this happy and relaxed. And that's saying something considering you and Torque are starting married life by adopting three children."

"I have no idea how I thought I'd be able to do it on my own. Torque is so good with them." Cassidy put both hands on her lower back and stretched.

"He must have had a good dad." Kelly pretended to be totally engrossed in deciding whether "Wonder" went into the pile for tweens or early teens, lest Cassidy realize that she was totally digging for info on Tough's childhood. *Not* because she was interested in him, because as an engaged woman, she was not, but because she was naturally curious about what caused certain people to grow up to be productive members of society and some to...not. If she hadn't majored in social work, she would have majored in psychology.

"No. Not even close. Come on, Kelly. What kind of parent names their child Torque?"

Not a normal one, for sure. If Cassidy were having a "normal" wedding, Kelly might have already met Tough. But Cassidy hadn't wanted a shower, and they were doing the wedding and reception as minimally as possible. Cassidy had said there was too much suffering in the world for her to waste money on putting on a big show. Torque, as far as Kelly could tell, only wanted Cassidy and didn't give a flip about the wedding.

"Doesn't he have a brother with an odd name?" Kelly asked in what she hoped was an offhand way.

"Yeah. Turbo."

No, not that one. "Another?"

"He has two other brothers, and you seem awfully curious. Why?"

Kelly shut her mouth. Cassidy was right. The tingle in her leg from the brush of his fingers, the excitement she felt at the idea of seeing him next week at the wedding, the security he brought to her psyche when she thought about renting the space next to him...she shouldn't be thinking of him at all. Let alone with such emotion. For some reason, she didn't even want to mention that he was fixing her car, like even talking about him might make Cassidy suspicious that Kelly was thinking about him way more than she should be.

The kids yelled and cheered, causing both Cassidy and Kelly to look over. Harris had dismissed them from the circle where she'd been reading to them, and they had run to the half-court that filled the other side of the big building opposite the study tables. Two teenagers were helping organize them into teams for a game of basketball.

Harris gathered her things up, along with her book, and hurried over, her long skirt flowing around her legs.

"Have you girls seen the latest?" she asked before she threw her stuff on a stool and grabbed her phone from her bag.

"The latest?" Kelly asked.

Cassidy rolled her eyes then focused on watching her small twins, making sure they weren't in the way of the kids who had started to dribble around the makeshift court. "The latest advice column. You know? The one plastered on billboards all over town?"

Kelly wrinkled her forehead. "Dr. T? The mechanic who only answers men's love questions?"

"Yes," Harris said with bright eyes before ducking her head and clicking on her phone again. "Ah!" she exclaimed. "Here it is!"

"I forgot today was Wednesday." Cassidy shook her head, but she grinned and moved to where she could look over Harris's shoulder.

"Totally understandable since you're mothering small children," Harris said without looking up.

"Well," Kelly said after a few minutes of silence. "Aren't you going to read it to us?" She took another bite of her cookie.

"I can read faster when I read to myself, and I have to see what he says today. He's so funny!"

"He is funny," Cassidy said, lifting one of her twins and offering her a cookie. "But his advice is always 100% accurate. I think the writer is actually a woman."

"Of course, it's a woman. Dr. Phil isn't even this astute," Harris said with a firm nod.

Cassidy raised a brow. "Thing is, he never offers advice to women. Only men."

"I've seen the billboards around here. Like he's a famous radio or TV personality. Is he based in Pennsylvania?" Kelly asked.

"I think he's out of LA," Harris said. "The big ones always are. Or New York."

"So, are you going to read it to us?" Kelly asked, despite her unbelief in the power of love that Dr. T seemed to promote.

Harris lifted her eyes and cleared her throat dramatically. "Okay, here goes: 'Dear Dr. T, My wife complains because I spend too much time in the garage. She wants me to help with dishes and crap like that. How can I tell her I'm busy? Thanks. -Working in my garage.'"

"Wow. The jerk needs to realize the wife can't do it all," Cassidy said.

"Yeah, his poor wife should be the one writing in." Kelly set the book down.

Harris's eyes were dancing. "Ready for his answer?"

"Sure. But there's no way I'm coming down in favor of the guy on this one," Kelly said.

"Me either," Cassidy agreed.

"'Dear Working, Sorry 'bout your luck, dude. But your wife works hard too. Give her the package of that sweet little something you bought her to wear and tell her if she meets you in the garage wearing it after you help her put the cherubs in bed and hands you your filter wrench while you change the oil, you'll do the dishes for a week. (Tip: take them out to the yard after she goes to work and hose them off. Make sure to get them back in the cupboard before she gets home.) Don't blame me if she announces Baby #3 a month from now.'"

Their laughter drew the attention of the kids playing ball. Harris shushed them. "Stop laughing, girls!"

"Do you think he's really going to do that?"

"The dishes? I hope not," Cassidy said.

"Of course, he's not. Although the idea of wearing lingerie in the garage..." Kelly almost slapped her hand over her mouth.

"Is not something you'll ever worry about," Cassidy said to her. "Preston probably doesn't even know how to lift the hood on that sporty thing he drives."

Kelly swallowed. Preston wasn't exactly the kind of guy who would do anything except park his car in the garage. Both of her friends were looking at her strangely. "To you, Cassidy. Torque's a mechanic." She grinned, hoping it looked real. "I'm definitely knocking before I walk into his garage from now on. I don't need to see your 'sweet little something.'"

"I'll have to make sure he sees this column. Although he doesn't have a problem helping with the kids." Cassidy grinned, a very unlawyerly grin. She nodded at Harris's phone. "No question about it, that guy is good." She nodded her head in appreciation, before sighing. "I'd better round up the kids and head out." She walked away, still smiling.

Harris clicked her phone off. "I so look forward to that column."

"You and half the country." Kelly set a book down in the correct pile.

"I think it's more than half." Harris spun a little, a dreamy smile on her face.

"It does seem to be the most popular thing going. Folks are so fed up with politics." Kelly kept her head down, pretending to study the book. Preston's head was always in politics. She grew tired of the constant arguing and rancor that being in politics seemed to entail.

"Yeah," Harris said. "Somehow Dr. T manages to find the bridge that spans our differences, rather than the river that divides them."

"And he always makes us laugh," Kelly admitted.

"True. Although we're saying 'he.' I'm almost positive he's a she." Harris's smile slipped.

"You could be right." Kelly picked at a lone crumb on the counter. What would it be like to be with a man who made her laugh or made her feel desirable? She shook those thoughts away. Preston was a great guy. They had a solid friendship. They really did love each other. She would be able to spend her life getting kids off the street and showing kids like Jasmine someone cared about them. She was lucky to have Preston and grateful for the support of his parents, especially his mother, who was almost like her mother too.

"Are you okay?" Harris asked.

Kelly jerked her head up. She hadn't realized that Harris had been studying her. Hopefully her thoughts hadn't been reflected on her face.

"Of course." She racked her brain for an excuse, just in case her face had shown more than it should have. "I was in an accident today."

"Oh, no! Why didn't you say so? Are you okay?" Harris laid a hand on her arm and searched her body like there would be blood she hadn't noticed before.

"I'm fine." Kelly held both hands up. "The older gentleman who hit me is fine too. My car...not so fine. And the man didn't want it turned in because he was afraid his kids would have his license taken away."

"So he's going to pay for it himself?"

She brushed the crumb off the counter and said as nonchalantly as possible, "It happened over on the south side, right in front of Tough Baxter's garage. He's doing the repairs."

"Then your car is in good hands." Harris's voice trailed off as one of Cassidy's twins started crying, and she hurried over to help.

"I know." Kelly looked at her phone. A couple of hours until it was time to take the kids back to their homes. The basketball game was winding down, and it'd be time to help with homework.

Maybe she'd stop by the new place after she dropped the kids off and look around a bit. Dream. After all, she wanted to be the biggest blessing she could be to as many children as possible. Finding this property was just the first step. She could spend some time enjoying it.

TOUGH LEANED against the side of the building. The streetlight was out, and the darkness enveloped him. There was a time, not that long ago, when he'd have been enjoying a cigarette right now while waiting for the paint on Mr. Hormell's car to dry. Smoking had been a stupid habit, taken up because it was the only thing he could do that wouldn't completely break his mother's heart if she'd still been living. Drinking was out of the question. And he'd promised that he wouldn't run around with lots of women like his dad, so he had made girls completely off-limits; it was the only way he knew to keep his promise. Drugs had never interested him. He'd seen too much of what they could do to a man. So smoking it was. An added benefit was that people didn't expect him to talk as much when he had a cancer stick hanging out of his mouth.

He'd quit. It hadn't been easy, and the urge still stole over him at times. Like now. Something to keep his hands and mouth busy, since Kelly had just walked around the corner. He couldn't actually see her in the dark, but there was no mistaking her scent which blew toward him on the early evening breeze. The scent which brought images of glitter and sunshine to his mind had been burned into his brain earlier in the day.

Her feet made little tapping noises on the cement. She must have gotten new shoes since he dropped her off at the center earlier this afternoon.

She stopped at the door to what would be "her" side of the warehouse, still a quarter block away from where he stood. She sighed. A soft whisper in the dark.

From experience, he knew he might be able to talk to her now. His tongue loosened after the sun went down and the lights went out. He never considered himself a creature of the night, but he definitely found it easier to talk when he couldn't see the person he spoke to. Or maybe when he thought the person couldn't see him. Yeah. He thought of his computer and his work on it. Definitely that was what made the difference. When he didn't feel like he was being watched, the words flowed easier.

The doorknob rattled. Kelly let out a frustrated whisper. It was locked; he'd made sure of it after she'd fallen into his office earlier. He tilted his head. Had she come back innocently looking at the building she'd agreed to rent? Or had she agreed to rent the building because she was onto him?

He dismissed the idea. After spending so much time watching her around town, he was sure she wasn't with the press. Almost sure.

Soft, slow clicks sounded on the sidewalk. They stopped after a few feet, like maybe she was peering into the door on his side of the building. The one he seldom used that went straight into his shop.

He shoved his hands into his pockets, and his voice came out raspy in the darkness. "Looking for something?"

She gasped and jumped. "Who are you? Where are you?"

Tough was surprised at the fear in her voice. He hadn't meant to scare her. His fingers closed around the lighter in his pocket. He pulled it out and snapped it on, holding it just in front of his chest so she could see his face.

With the light in front of him, he lost even her outline. He didn't hear her shoes click either, so her voice beside him was a shock.

"Tough."

He snapped the light off. Since she would be renting beside him, he figured he'd have more chances to have a conversation with her, but he hadn't expected it to be tonight. If he had even a glimmer of being able to say a few words, the light had to go. He couldn't see her, but she could see him, and it would mess with his head. Like his head wasn't already messed up.

"Why don't you like me?" she asked, her voice husky, with an earthy tone he found almost as irresistible as her scent.

She thought he didn't like her. "I don't?"

"Why?" she insisted.

He'd meant it as a question. His inflection skills were undoubtedly rusty. He crossed his arms over his chest and leaned against the wall.

He tried again, trying to put the right inflection in it. "I don't."

He felt more than saw her lean against the wall beside him.

"Is Mr. Hormell's car done?"

Yeah, that was better. He could talk about cars easily in the dark. "One more coat."

"Oh, good." She shifted, and her scent became stronger. "I'm renting the other side, so I guess we'll see each other a lot."

"Hmm."

"I'm going to be having some remodeling done. It'll be a couple weeks before I move in. But I'll have kids running around. I hope that's not going to be a problem?"

There was no problem. Not with her. Not with having kids running around. All summer, there were kids out. He'd never kicked anyone out of his shop.

"I'm a little worried about some of them. They all come from bad backgrounds. There didn't used to be so much easy access to drugs in the area, but I've seen so many problems with opioids." She paused, giving a soft sigh. He could just see the faint outline of her hand, fingering her purse strap. Just hear the whisper of movement. "I've heard of how beneficial it is to have children mixed in with senior citizens...that's one of the benefits if I do this without government money. I can use real-time knowledge about what works and doesn't and shift things as I see fit—like opening a center here. If I have to go through the government red tape, it will take forever, and the place will be rented out."

It would, because if she'd waited another week, he would've had the money.

She went on a little more about her hopes and dreams for the kids and seniors. The husky note faded out as she got more into the plans she had. He missed the huskiness but still enjoyed listening to her thoughts. After a half an hour where she barely came up for breath, and he was sure the paint was dry, she finally stopped and gave a small laugh.

"I guess I've talked your ear off." She laughed again. "When you work with kids, you don't usually get a chance to have a captive audience. You're easy to talk to." She straightened from the side of the building where she'd been leaning. The disappointment pooling in his stomach surprised him.

He needed to go paint that car. Typically, he didn't dally when it came to jobs. But he'd enjoyed this time, in the dark, with Kelly. She was engaged—he couldn't forget—but that didn't mean he couldn't like listening to her.

She stood close enough to him that he could see her outline, and it hadn't moved. He waited. He'd leave when she did.

A sigh whispered through the darkness. "I guess I'm feeling restless," she said softly.

"We all do at some point," Tough said, surprised at how easily the words came out. He didn't know what she was feeling restless about— her work, her fiancé, her life in general—but wished he had the words to ask.

"The feeling goes away, I guess."

"Yeah." And like he'd done all his life, he just waited. Maybe she'd tell.

"My friend Cassidy is getting married. Well, you know. It's to your brother. I keep forgetting that."

"Yeah."

"I should be planning my own wedding."

Her fiancé had a pile of money, and she'd be set for life. She'd be able to rent a hundred warehouses to turn into kids' play areas. If Tough were a better person, he'd be happy about that and not have this hope in his chest that Kelly would dump her new rich fiancé. He clicked the lighter in his pocket. Dump the fiancé and what? Fall in love with the poor-as-dirt mechanic and body guy who couldn't string a sentence together in her presence and could never provide her with everything she wanted?

She sighed. "You know, I didn't put it together right away today, but I remember you from first grade." Turning toward him, she touched his arm. Cool fingers against his hot skin. "Do you?"

A little grin hovered over his lips. "You were getting married back then, too."

She laughed. Little bells in the darkness. "Yep. The Marrying Game was the big thing on the playground. I was the last holdout in our group, and my friends were making me get married."

"You didn't want to."

"They were dragging me to the 'altar.'"

He snorted. "One bridesmaid had a hold of each arm."

Her voice held a smile. "Yep. And Chance Detweiler was waiting at the fence to say 'I do.' But you came over and said that I ought to get to choose who I wanted."

"Is that what I said?"

"I wouldn't forget. Because for some reason, even for the game, even at that age, I couldn't say words I didn't mean. Not words that serious."

Even back then, he couldn't take his eyes off her. And couldn't stand for her to be "marrying" someone else. Even if it was a first-grade game.

"I'm not sure why, but I remember that, and I remember that you took me to the Fitzsimmonses' house after school that day. You told me she wanted a little girl and she'd probably take me."

"She brought my mom some soup." His mom had been in bed, sick from the cancer treatments. Mrs. Fitzsimmons had been doing her "good deed" by taking the poor neighbor soup. "She said she only had a son and she longed for a little girl to dress up and have tea parties with."

"You took me to her house."

He couldn't believe that it had never entered his little first-grade mind that the lady might not want Kelly.

"She took me."

"Yeah." Tough leaned his head back against the building and looked up at the stars. She'd taken Kelly all right. Taken her in and almost raised her like a daughter. Not quite like a daughter, since her son was now engaged to Kelly.

Through the glow from the city, he could still see a few brave stars, shining through. Would he have still taken Kelly to Mrs. Fitzsimmons if he'd known he was effectively giving her away to another guy? Immediately he knew he would have. Even in first grade, Tough hadn't had any thoughts that he was good enough for Kelly. Even when she was as dirty and scruffy as him. He admired her. He might even have a little crush on her, but he wasn't under any illusions that there was any kind of future for them.

"That changed my life." The husky note was back in her voice.

It had changed his too, since Mrs. Fitzsimmons had paid for Kelly to be transferred to the most exclusive private school in the city, and he'd barely seen her again.

"You didn't talk to me then any more than you talk now."

"Didn't need to."

"All you said was you knew someone who wanted me." She laughed, a sweet bell-like sound on the night air. "That's all I needed to hear. Surprisingly you were right, and my whole life changed." She shifted, and her hand landed on his arm again. This time, it stayed. "You know, that's what I've wanted to do ever since. What you did that day—take kids who don't have any hope. Who don't have anyone to love them. And give them what you gave me." She laughed, maybe at the irony. "As an adult woman, I want to be what you were in first grade. Someday."

He turned, grabbing her wrist, and whispered fiercely, "You're better. Better than I ever was. Better than anyone else. You care about these kids, you truly do. You're making a difference."

"No one understands why I need to. Why this is what I want. *All* I want."

He didn't have to think about it. "It's because any of those kids could have been you."

"*Should* have been me."

"No. You were meant for more." He pushed away from the wall.

"They are too."

"And you're going to see they get the opportunities to reach their potential."

"It's my dream. That has always been my dream. I always gave the Fitzsimmonses credit, but I realized today that it was you, too. I would never have met Mrs. Fitzsimmons if it hadn't been for you."

There was truth in her statement. But he'd just been a first grader who saw two needs and met them. Not a big deal.

"I didn't make you who you are, and neither did the Fitzsimmonses. You had opportunities, and you made the best of them. *Because* of who you are."

Her breath blew over his face, and he realized he was still grasping her wrist. He let go. She didn't move. It was hard to tell, since he couldn't see much, but her breath seemed to come in little gasps.

"You believe in me. But you don't even know me." She bit her lip, her white teeth flashing in the dark. "You didn't rescue any of the other girls when they had to get married. Just me."

"Just you." He echoed her words, like he was agreeing, even though implicit in her tone was the question, "Why?" But he couldn't answer that. Couldn't say why he'd watched the Marrying Game from the side of the playground where he played trucks with the rest of his buddies and didn't give a flip about the other girls getting "married." There were even some who didn't want to and had been dragged down the aisle, laughing and protesting, just like Kelly. But he hadn't considered going to their defense. He'd only watched to make sure Kelly wasn't getting married. When it had been her turn, all he'd needed to see was that she didn't want to, and he'd gone over, having no idea of what he was going to say or do. And, although there were always children whose parents neglected them, he hadn't considered taking anyone but Kelly to Mrs. Fitzsimmons. Why? He didn't know.

"Why?" she finally whispered when he didn't say anything.

"I'd better get this car done." He fingered the lighter in his pocket. Sure, he admired Kelly. Liked her. There was even this little crazy attraction. But that's all it could be. Trying to examine his feelings, even the feelings of a first grader—there was no point in that.

She stepped back, and the longing for a cigarette hit him hard. Not for the nicotine craving but for something to do with his hands, his mouth. A distraction from what he wanted to do, which was keep her from backing away from him.

"Yeah. It's late. I'm sure my fiancé will be calling me any time."

Her words hit him like a hammer to his thumb. Exactly the way she intended for them to hit, he assumed. But he couldn't just let her walk off into the darkness.

"I'll walk you to your car."

"That's not necessary."

"Then I'll walk to the corner and watch until you get in."

"I'm not a child."

"No." He certainly wasn't confused about that. "But it's late and these streets aren't safe."

"I'm on these streets all the time. I just dropped kids off two blocks over. Plus..." She moved, rustling in her purse, he assumed. "I have this." She held something up.

Pulling the lighter out of his pocket, he flicked it on. "A rabbit's foot?"

"A *lucky* rabbit's foot."

She had a lucky rabbit's foot. He couldn't stop the smile that turned the corners of his mouth up. Crazy woman. "You don't actually believe that's going to keep you safe?"

"Not because it's magical, exactly," she said with a saucy tone. "But, come on. Who's going to hurt someone who's waving a rabbit's foot around?"

He grunted, which, to his surprise, was almost a laugh. "I'll visit you in the psych ward."

"That's not funny."

"I was being serious. I can see it now. Gang members capturing you and turning you in, because the streets aren't safe with a psycho like you on the loose."

"Wow. I had no idea you had such an overactive imagination."

"Hey, criminals have feelings too."

"You just switched sides! Defending the criminals. You are definitely not walking me to my car."

This time he did laugh, a short, rusty sound. He reached out in the dark and took her elbow. "I'm always on your side, Kelly. Come on. Let me walk you to your car because I like you and it's fun to walk in the dark with a pretty girl." Not that he would know or anything.

She moved easily with the pressure on her elbow. "You like me? How come you weren't talking to me earlier?"

No. No secret sharing. Not with anyone, but especially not with Kelly.

They made it to the corner and the edge of the streetlight before she spoke again. "You clammed up on me again?"

He ignored the question. There was no answer for it anyway. "That your rental?" He nodded at the sleek muscle car that looked very out of place along the cracked and broken sidewalk.

"It's my fiancé's spare."

There he was again. Between them. As he should be. "Nice wheels." Far nicer than anything he'd ever be able to offer Kelly. She deserved every nice thing.

She shrugged. "It starts when I turn the key. I'm not picky about anything else."

"Heat? AC?"

She laughed. "Okay. That's true. A good heater and AC in the summer." Her phone buzzed in her purse, and she dug it out. "I'm good. I know you have a car to finish. Thanks for being the bunny foot backup."

Tough waited. He wasn't walking until she was in her car driving away.

She glanced at her phone, and her face fell.

# Chapter Five

Preston had finally decided to text her back. He'd been okay with the accident, as she'd known he would. But she'd also mentioned the warehouse she had agreed to rent, not thinking he would have a problem with it. She hadn't expected this. She blinked and read the text again.

> I would appreciate it if you focus on planning our wedding. Everyone in the Asian delegation has their spouse with them. The new activity center for the kids can wait.

She sighed. They'd tried several times to get a date pinned down for their wedding before he left, although she had never formally accepted his offer. It was more Mrs. Fitzsimmons who was pushing for it. She'd worn the ring, wanting it to feel right. It didn't. The heaviness that descended on her didn't feel right either. It had been several weeks, and nothing felt right.

She punched into her phone, ignoring her gut.

> Tell me what date suits you, and I'll get it done. I can do both.

It wasn't long before her phone dinged with an answer.

> No. The wedding is the priority. I want it to be spectacular.

She bit back a sigh as her fingers flew over the keys.

> It will be. That's what I do.

> Talk to my mom. She'll help you.

> Of course. I wouldn't do it without her.

> Spend as much as you need to. I want to get the wedding going, and I don't want you to overextend yourself. Save the world AFTER we're married.

Ignoring the icky stickiness in her chest, she typed back,

> I won't.

Now what? She wasn't going to quit working on the new activity center just because Preston wanted her to. But she had kind of thought she'd have his support and they could talk about it. They hadn't always talked about everything—he was a very busy man—but he always had great ideas, and she loved that she wasn't alone.

She dropped her phone back into her purse and dug for her key.

She hadn't realized Tough was still there until he asked, "Everything okay?"

Her heart jumped, and she put a hand on her chest before turning. "You startled me." He stood back in the shadows, out of the glow of the streetlights. She squinted to see him.

"Everything okay?" he repeated. His voice was gravelly and deep and, coming out of the darkness like it was, should have been uncomfortable. But it wrapped around her like a comfortable sweatshirt. That was Tough. Unpretentious as an old sweatshirt.

"It's fine."

He crossed his arms over his chest and waited.

She rattled the keys in her hand. "Fine. Preston wants me to plan our wedding, and he doesn't want me renting this building." She gritted her teeth. Not being born with a silver spoon in her mouth had imparted a fair amount of grit to her personality. Giving up wasn't something she did well or often.

"Preston tells you what to do?"

"Preston *pays* for what I do." That wasn't entirely true. Her car had been a gift last Christmas, and of course, he'd picked out and paid for the heavy engagement ring on her finger, but so far, he'd not funded anything for her. He had, however, given generously to her charitable activities. His family had a ton of investments, including a large online media conglomerate, and did give large amounts to charity.

Every time over the past twelve years they'd talked about what a great power couple they'd make, he'd said how she would be the perfect political spouse because of all her charities. She assumed he'd want to help fund them.

"Or doesn't pay?" Tough said, with a small emphasis on "doesn't."

"It's not really a matter of paying. He wants me to focus on the wedding."

"You can't do both?"

"Of course I can." The words came out with more frustration attached than she meant to allow. It was a temporary thing, happening only until they were married. Preston really was very generous, and he certainly wasn't a control freak. They'd had an easy friendship for years and an unspoken agreement that they'd be perfect together. She twisted the ring on her finger. It was a spoken agreement now, she supposed, even if the ring didn't feel right on her hand.

"He just doesn't want me to 'overextend' myself." She used her fingers to do air quotes.

"Hmm."

She waited, but Tough didn't say anymore. "What? You think he's right?"

"You were planning on his money to rent here?"

"I was planning on his money to keep me from having to go through the government red tape." It's not like she was thinking tens of thousands of dollars. "I have enough to rent it but not enough to renovate it, too. Usually I get started on a project, and Preston eventually notices and offers to help. His help is typically monetary." The idea of Preston with a hammer in his hand was laughable. "But if he wants me to focus on our wedding, he's not going to be 'helping.'"

"And now?"

At that question, her starch disappeared, and she slumped against the car, facing Tough. "I'm going to figure that out." Somehow.

Time ticked by. A car drove slowly up the street. She didn't turn to look but could almost feel Tough's interest as he watched. Probably to make sure it wasn't going to cause any harm to her. Something about that loosened some of the tightness in her chest. She was sure that Preston wanted her to focus on the wedding because that's what he wanted. It had nothing to do with overextending herself. Tough, on the other hand, truly seemed interested in protecting her for her sake.

"You have other avenues?" he asked, once the car disappeared from sight.

"I can try to go through the community center and the children's charity. But both of those have boards and budgets and won't be a quick solution. I was planning on doing this myself because then I have the freedom to make it what I want without getting a bunch of other people involved. Other opinions are nice, but the more people that are involved, the more unwieldly the process gets."

"I see."

"Cassidy would probably fund me." But she was planning a wedding scheduled for next weekend. Kelly couldn't bother her now.

She might be able to put together a charity gala, but it would take time and money up front. Preston probably wouldn't be okay with that.

But the kids on this side of town needed a place where they could be supported and helped without being carted across town. She had to make it work, and she would do so, for the kids.

"I can help."

"What?" She lifted her head and squinted. He still stood out of the light, leaning against the building with his arms crossed over his chest. "You'll help? How?" She bit back a laugh at the thought of Tough in a tux helping her host a charity gala. Nope. Not going to happen.

"I have money for the rent."

"I need a security deposit and two months' rent." Plus money for renovations. Which she had maybe half. But maybe if she put his money together with hers, it would give her time to plan some kind of charity fundraiser to raise the rest...

"I said I have it." His tone didn't change.

Kelly tilted her head. "I can borrow it?"

"No."

She almost rolled her eyes. Why tell her he had it if he wasn't going to help her?

"I'm giving it to you."

"No." The refusal sprang automatically to her lips.

Without moving, he asked, "Do you want the check now, or do you want to come back for it tomorrow?"

"I'm not taking your money."

"Okay. I'll write the check out to Mr. Millard."

"I'll pay you back."

"Maybe you're not the only person in the world who wants to see the kids have a place to hang out and play and to see them being taken care of by people who care about them?"

It was the longest he'd ever spoken at one time. Kelly closed her mouth. She didn't want to insult him by calling him poor, and she didn't want to question his judgment by telling him he couldn't afford to give her so much. But the fact was he was poor and couldn't afford to give her that much money. If he were making tons of money, he'd have a garage in the best part of town, a new tow truck, and lots of employees. Obviously, he was still working to get his business off the ground, and she wasn't going to jeopardize that.

"I appreciate the kind gesture, but let me see what I can do on my end, first."

He pushed off the wall and took two languid steps toward her. He shoved his hands in his pockets as though to keep from grabbing her. His eyes narrowed and locked on her shoulder.

"You need the money. I offered it. What's the problem?"

She twisted the keys in her hand and looked away.

"You'll take Preston's money without a qualm, but mine isn't good enough? Is it because I earned it working with these?" He pulled his hands, black grease-stained and dirty, out of his pockets and held them up.

Fine. He was going to get all huffy about it. Well, he wasn't going to intimidate her. She would tell him the truth. She took two steps forward and leaned over, trying to snag his gaze. "Look at me." She crossed her arms over her chest and waited.

His eyes, all warm walnut swirl, bounced to hers before twisting away. His shoulders rose, like he was taking a deep breath. A muscle in his eye jumped and popped, but he narrowed them and slammed her with his gaze.

She gasped. Her hand went to her chest as though to stop her heart from jumping out. All the thoughts in her head disappeared as she looked into his eyes. Swirled browns, warm and dark, looked back at her.

How long had she stood there? It felt like years as time ticked by both fast and slow. She was supposed to be saying something, but she couldn't find the words, couldn't remember what had just been so important.

"You had something to tell me?" he asked. The words came out deep and low, rolling over her like a soft caress, sending small electric shocks down her back.

She ripped her gaze away and took a moment to gather herself. That reaction was unexpected. Unprecedented. Shocking. Her heart was still not beating normally, and her stomach had knotted like an old pine tree. But she needed to speak.

Clearing her throat, she said as forcefully as she could, ineffective since she couldn't find the courage to look him in those polished walnut eyes again, "You can't afford to give that money to me."

"Isn't that my call?" he asked in the same low tone.

She crossed her arms over her chest. "I won't allow you to give away what you need."

"If you were my wife, we'd make the decision together. Since you're not, you don't get input."

Her lungs froze at the word "wife."

He kept talking. "I'm writing a check out to Mr. Millard tomorrow."

"It still needs to be fixed up." She had some money but not enough.

"I'll help."

"What?"

"You get it rented. I'll help you fix it up."

She forced herself to look at him, but he wasn't staring into her eyes anymore, and she couldn't find the words to argue anyway.

"Now, get in your car and drive. I've got a car to finish, but I'm not doing it until you're safely away." His eyes met hers for several fleeting moments, and she saw more than she expected in the mahogany depths.

She turned, got in her car, and drove away.

# Chapter Six

Tough sipped his coffee and tried to concentrate on the potential questions that had been sent in. Several of his syndications, as well as all his advertisers, were begging him to publish more than once a week. He could do it; he might even be able to publish daily, and that would provide more than triple the income, which would enable him to do more repair work for the elderly for free, which is what he did with the money from the column—bought parts, then donated his time doing what he loved for older people on a fixed income. Who was he kidding? He donated to anyone who couldn't afford it.

He had enough readers, enough interest, enough men writing in... He enjoyed the column. It started off as a mechanical advice column, just something for him to do in the evening or on slow days when he didn't have any work in the garage. Somehow his advice hadn't been limited to cars. And men seemed to appreciate his mechanical analogies, while women loved the way he didn't hold back in telling the men they were wrong. Years of standing in the shadows, watching, had taught him more than most people learned by experience. When a person watched, they saw both sides. Still, if people found out that he was a mechanic with absolutely no life experience—he'd never even had a girlfriend, let alone any kind of married relationship, and he certainly didn't have a psychology degree—well, he didn't want to think about that.

Back in the day, his column had been named Tough Talk. But somehow, it'd gotten shortened to T and someone had stuck a "Dr." on the front of it. Dr. T. Ha. If they only knew.

If Kelly knew...

Would she think he was ridiculous for daring to write a relationship advice column? Probably. No one else in his life ever believed he could be more than a mechanic/body guy. The fact that he owned his own shop pretty much shocked everyone who knew him. Like if someone doesn't say much, they're automatically considered stupid.

He shook his head and went back to trying to read the questions that had been emailed in overnight, trying to find one that would resonate with the most readers. And one that he could answer. Some of the questions he really did have no clue about.

Finally, he settled on one: What can I do to get my wife interested in me again?

He answered it then announced to his blog followers that, starting next week, his column would be published daily and that this Friday would see a bonus column.

He clicked the computer off just as the garage door banged open.

Walking out of the office, Tough carefully shut the door behind him. Maybe Kelly wouldn't care about his side job, and it certainly shouldn't matter to him whether she did or not. But he wasn't taking the chance of her finding out. Not until he could think on it more and decide if she'd think he was a fake and a fraud.

Mr. Sigel hunched over his cane, walking slowly over to the near wall where Tough had his coffee maker set up, along with plenty of cups and other supplies. The old men who hung around the garage all day needed plenty of coffee and their checkerboard. Gossip just wasn't as good without those supporting characters.

"Tough. You out of bed already?" Mr. Sigel paused in his shuffle and looked up, his bushy brows sticking out like awnings over intense blue eyes.

"Slept with my boots on, sir," Tough replied with a serious face that didn't fool Mr. Sigel.

"When I was your age, I had a half-day of work in by this time in the morning."

Tough poured coffee into a cup. Mr. Sigel drank it black. "Kids nowadays," Tough said, shaking his head and handing the cup to Mr. Sigel.

"Carry it for me," Mr. Sigel said. "I'm getting my spot on the black side before Alfred comes in and takes it, like he did on Tuesday."

Things had definitely gotten interesting on Tuesday, that was for sure. Tough followed Mr. Sigel's shuffle over to the checkerboard.

"Why aren't there any cars in here? You slacking?" He stopped shuffling and looked up. "Or is work slow?" Those blue eyes that provided a window to the intelligence lurking in the eighty-year-old brain narrowed on Tough. "You come on hard times, boy?"

Tough shook his head and glanced at his watch. "It's only 7:30. Plus, what's that?" He nodded over at Kelly's car. Mr. Sigel had already seen it, he was sure. The old man just constantly worried about him having enough work.

Tough didn't mention that he'd been up until two, since he'd finished Mr. Hormell's car then went and picked him up at the hotel, waited for Mr. Hormell to get ready, took the man out to the all-night diner for a meal, then brought him here and sent him off.

"When I was a boy..." The garage door banged open again, cutting Mr. Siegel's statement off. Not that Tough hadn't heard it a hundred times.

Alfred strode in. Younger than Mr. Siegel by fifteen years, Alfred was the youngest of Tough's "regulars."

"Morning, Tough."

"Alfred." Tough nodded, hiding his smile as Mr. Siegel hustled the rest of the way to the black side of the checkerboard, carrying his cane.

Alfred poured a half-cup of coffee. He filled the cup the rest of the way up with cream. "Mr. Siegel has the black today, I see," he said before lifting the cup to his lips.

"The early bird gets the worm," Mr. Siegel said. It always amazed Tough how good Mr. Siegel's hearing was when someone was talking about him. At all other times, he could hardly hear a thing.

Alfred pulled the newspaper out from under his arm. "I'd have been here earlier, but the paperboy slept in again."

"When I was a boy," Mr. Siegel began.

Alfred stepped over and cut him off with a comment of his own. Tough was glad they were distracted, since the door banged open once again—he really needed to take it off its hinges and shave an eighth of an inch off the bottom so it fit in the frame—and Kelly blew in.

She wore pink today. Her dress flowed around her in a cloud, her earrings and bracelets clacked, and her blond hair bobbed and swayed.

Tough wanted to tell her how beautiful she looked. How fresh and pretty and totally out of place in his dark, dirty garage. But, of course, in the harsh light of day, his tongue twisted and unhinged from his brain. So, he crossed his arms over his chest, planted his feet, and waited.

"Tough! I've thought about it, and I wanted to apologize for being stubborn last night. If you still want to donate the money to rent the garage..."

Mr. Siegel cleared his throat, much louder than he normally did. The sound brought Kelly up short, and she twisted. The two men had both risen to their feet when she walked in. "Oh, I didn't realize you had customers."

"We're not customers. Carry on," Alfred said in the voice he used only for ladies. At least, that was the voice Tough assumed he was using. Tough had never actually heard that tone from him before.

"Um..." Kelly looked from the men to Tough and back to the men. "You can sit back down?"

Both men nodded their heads and sat down but did not resume their game or their argument. His personal life was usually as interesting as watching rocks bake in the sun on the sidewalk. Apparently both men assumed it was about to get a lot more interesting. If only.

Kelly turned back to Tough. She lowered her voice. "Am I interrupting something?"

"No." Thankfully, his tongue cooperated. "They're regulars." Hard to believe but he got another two words out, even if he couldn't meet her eyes.

"Regulars? Like this is a restaurant, too?"

"No."

"Stop that!" she hissed and planted her hands on her hips.

Tough raised his brows.

She motioned with her hand. "You were talking to me last night. Don't even start acting like you hate me this morning."

"I don't." He raised his hands, ignoring his eye tic.

"I know. We established that last night."

They had?

"You don't hate me; you tolerate me. You are not allowed to slide backward."

Wow. No wonder so many men wrote in with relationship problems. Tough had no idea that they'd established anything last night other than he was paying for her rent.

"Tough. You're doing it again."

He wanted to run his hand through his hair in frustration, but he resisted. He might not be able to control his tongue, but he could have everything else under complete command.

"Fine." She gave a small, sad smile that said it was anything but fine and fingered the strap on her purse. "If you're still offering the rent, I'll take it. I ran it by my boss on the phone this morning, and it was just like I knew it would be—a probable yes, but not for several months. After Christmas, at the earliest. I don't want to wait that long, there are kids that need saving now." She blew a hair out of her face and brushed a hand down her dress. "Also, I want to know how much the repairs for my car are going to be."

"No charge."

She froze. Her eyes flew to his face. He met her gaze briefly, feeling the charge fling through his body, down to his work boots, and back up, before he looked over her shoulder.

"I said I would pay."

"I said no charge."

"A thousand dollars?" She took a step closer.

"No charge." He held his ground, keeping his arms crossed over his chest, as though for protection.

"Two thousand?" She stepped even closer.

"No charge." He refused to back up.

"Tell me how much I owe you," she said through gritted teeth.

"No. Charge." He looked down, managing to focus on her nose. Which was directly under his. Her enticing scent flirted with him each time he drew a breath. She was close enough that he could see the tiny freckles that arched over her cheeks. Her long lashes. The deep blue of her eyes, which reminded him of fresh blueberries on a summer morning. His eye ticked, and he didn't bother to try to hide it. She was angry, and an eye tic wasn't going to make her hate him more.

"When my wife looked at me like that, I'd grab her and kiss her," Alfred said, shocking Tough. He'd forgotten there was anyone else in the universe save Kelly and him. His eyes dropped to her lips. The urge that stole over his back and shoulders, pushing from the inside out, took him by surprise. He'd never been this tempted to lean down...

"Maybe that's what killed her," Mr. Sigel said irreverently.

Tough bit back a snort.

Kelly's lips twitched.

"I don't know what's become of this generation. Didn't anyone ever teach you the lady deserves respect?" Alfred asked, ignoring Mr. Sigel completely.

Tough's mouth dropped. "I am!"

"No, you're not, you little whippersnapper. Your arms are crossed, and you're arguing. Now, there is a time and a place for a good argument. No doubt. Mostly for the benefits of making up." Mr. Siegel lifted his hat and scratched his mostly bald head. "But you haven't caught her yet. It's been a while since I wooed my Annie, but come on, boy, don't be obtuse. You don't fight with her before you've caught her."

"I'm not trying to catch her," Tough said in exasperation.

"I'm not a fish," Kelly said in the same exasperated tone.

Tough's lips lifted; he couldn't help it. He tweaked her skirt. "That thing is pretty bulky. You could be hiding some fins under there."

"No! No!" Mr. Sigel said, his tone even more exasperated than Tough's and Kelly's had been. "You don't ever say she looks like a fish." He grabbed his cane and pretended to use it as he proceeded to shuffle over at a speed Tough had only hitherto seen him use when he thought his position at the checker table was in danger. "Listen, miss." Mr. Sigel grabbed her arm. "Tough really is a great guy. Just because he sleeps in his boots and disappears behind his computer for hours..."

Kelly's eyes snapped to Tough. Tough tried to interrupt—he didn't need Mr. Sigel giving away how he really made his living—but Mr. Sigel put a hand up. "You go home. Let me work on Tough here, teach him how to woo the women, and you come back in a week. I'd hate to see Tough lose out because he's a clod around girls. I've never met a finer man." He slapped Tough on the arm. "At least from his generation." He nodded. "He works hard, and he makes good coffee. Pays his bills on time and keeps his shop clean. No drugs. No alcohol." He tapped Tough's shirt pocket where, for the past ten years, his last, unsmoked cigarette peeked out. "This is just for show."

"No. It's a test of my willpower. Every day." He pulled the lighter out of his pocket and clicked it before shoving it back in. Kelly's eyes widened then narrowed, and her jaw dropped. Tough faced Mr. Sigel. "Thanks. She's engaged."

"When did you do that?" He turned. "Hey, Alfred," he shouted, although Alfred had moseyed over, like this was a rock concert and he was standing in the aisle to get a better view, holding his coffee cup. "Did you know Tough was engaged?"

"*She's* engaged. Not to me."

Mr. Sigel stopped. His mouth formed a perfect "O." He looked at Tough. Then Kelly. Then back to Tough. He looked at Kelly again.

This time when he spoke, his voice was low and sincere. "This boy would work himself into the ground for you. There isn't anyone better." He started to turn and leaned toward Tough. "I saw the way you looked at her when she walked in. It's the way I looked at my wife up until they closed the casket." He shuffled off, his cane making muted thumps on the cement.

Silence expanded and filled the garage. Tough's cheeks were hot, but he hoped his naturally dark complexion hid the blush.

Alfred took a sip of coffee and nodded thoughtfully. "I think this is the first time in seven years that I agree with Mr. Sigel. About all of it." He looked at Kelly when he spoke. She bit her lip and looked away.

She shifted awkwardly while Tough planted his feet on the floor, refusing to allow himself to show his embarrassment. What did two old guys know anyway?

He took a breath. "You can give me a check—"

"I don't have to pay you—"

Kelly laughed, a nervous, uncomfortable laugh, as they spoke at the same time.

Tough hated that she was nervous and uncomfortable. Such a change from the feisty confidence she'd displayed when she walked in. How could he get that back? If only his tongue would work long enough to make a joke. For Kelly, he'd try.

"You never did answer me about the fins you're hiding somewhere under there."

She blinked. Then smiled. He considered it a win.

"They come out after dark."

"Figured. Like a piranha." He held his hands up. "I'll quit arguing."

"That's the safe decision." She grinned and pulled her purse off her arm. "Now, do you take credit cards, or do I need to write a check?"

Tough swallowed. His computer was shut off, but his column would come up when he turned it on. "It's a little early for my credit card machine. A check would be easier."

She tilted her head. "You won't rip it up?"

"Probably not." He walked over to the counter where the coffee maker was. "Help yourself. It's not the fancy stuff, and it doubles as a degreaser."

"Huh?"

"I was kidding." Mostly. "It's strong."

"Oh."

"You can leave the check there." He named a figure. Lowballed. "If it's more than that, I'll let you know. I'm going over to start on this vehicle. Some lady conveniently wrecked her car right in front of my shop yesterday. Good for business."

"Ha. I bet."

Did she look disappointed as he walked away? He couldn't tell for sure.

"Hey, Tough?"

He stopped and turned. "Yeah?"

"If I get things worked out with Mr. Millard, will you really help renovate it?"

"You bet we will," Alfred interrupted.

Tough nodded. "He was a contractor before he retired."

Alfred shook his head. "Worst decision of my life."

"To be a contractor?" Tough asked in surprise.

"No. To retire."

"What's she putting over there?" Mr. Sigel asked.

"I'm going to make it a children's activity center," Kelly answered as though he'd been talking to her.

Mr. Sigel stomped his cane on the floor. "Just great. A bunch of noisy, undisciplined kids."

"Just like you used to be," Tough teased gently. "Just like I used to be."

"Yeah. Until I took you in hand and beat some sense into you."

Kelly looked shocked, but Tough just shrugged. He'd needed a firm hand. A firmer hand that his tough, old grandmother could apply. She did her best, but sometimes a boy just needed a man. Mr. Sigel had been that for him.

He shrugged. "Guess there's some other boys who need the same thing."

"Seems to go with the gender," Mr. Sigel said.

Kelly snorted. Tough walked toward her car, a smile warming his heart. Who knew making that special woman laugh would make him feel so good?

# Chapter Seven

Kelly pulled into the First Presbyterian Church for the wedding rehearsal. There was a small parking lot around back, but it seemed like everyone had parked out front, so she pulled in there, too.

Her phone rang. Finally. Preston.

"Hello?"

"Hey, I don't have much time, but you keep texting me to call you, so I'm calling."

She had wanted to talk about their relationship. Talk about how much it bothered her that it was weighing like an anchor around her neck. But that was a conversation she didn't want to rush. Should she wait?

"Well, I kind of wanted to talk to you."

"And?"

"How much time do you have?" This whole trip was extremely important to him. She didn't want to hold him up.

"About three minutes. I'm on the plane. They've already told us to shut our phones off. Listen, how about I try to call later?"

"Okay. It's not that important anyway, I guess." Was this the way normal couples worked? Would Preston make time for her if he really "loved" her? He was pretty pragmatic. Would he ever miss the lack of warmth in their relationship? The lack of sparks?

She said goodbye to Preston as she walked into the cool vestibule. She'd tried to text him about their own wedding, but he didn't want to have much to do with the planning. In the last two weeks since he'd basically commanded her to get it done, he'd helped her pick the date. That was it. She didn't figure he'd care about the reception halls that she'd narrowed down to three choices. But she felt like she needed to ask anyway. She didn't really care about having a big shindig, but she supposed that was part of her keeping her part of their bargain.

Her phone buzzed.

> The plane is leaving the terminal. Turning my phone off. I'll text you when we land.

She read the text and stuffed the phone in her purse. It would be early tomorrow morning before they landed in Paris where he'd catch another flight to Southeast Asia.

Shoving away the thought of Preston and all the issues that dredged up for her, she pushed through the heavy wood doors and into the massive sanctuary.

"She's here!" Jamal, older brother to Cassidy's twins, came running toward her. She threw a smile on her face, shoving aside the lingering feeling of impending doom that descended every time she tried to talk to Preston about their wedding.

Kneeling, she allowed Jamal to jump into her arms. His twin sisters came toddling along behind him. She wrapped them all in a hug, while they chattered about everything that had happened before she got there.

She stood, holding a twin's hand in each of her own, and started walking toward where the bridal party was gathered at the front of the church.

Cassidy stood, straight and regal, beside her fiancé, Torque. She was talking to Harris but threw Kelly a wave. Kelly nodded and smiled, her eyes scanning the rest of the wedding party.

A man caught her eye for just a second, and she thought he might be Tough, but she dismissed him almost immediately since he was engaged in a very animated conversation with the minister. The man of the cloth was roaring with laughter, doubling over, while the man who looked similar to Tough kept waving his arms and talking. Even the very serious-looking fellow in the glasses beside them smiled.

Definitely not Tough. She'd never seen him that vibrant. Not that she'd been back to the garage much in the last week. Once to talk to him about the renovations and once to tell him that they could start next week. Just yesterday, she'd ordered the supplies.

He'd delivered her car and brought the keys into her downtown social services office just three days after the accident. He'd looked out of place and uncomfortable in the fluorescent lights surrounded by sleek, modern designs. He hadn't stayed long. She didn't know how he'd gotten back to the garage, because he'd fled before she could offer him a ride.

Even though Cassidy had come from money, the wedding was not going to be over the top. She'd requested no showers or bachelorette parties since she didn't need anything.

Everything was geared to the kids she and Torque were adopting.

Cassidy looked at Torque again as the little girls dragged her closer. He'd been in prison but didn't look like an ex-con. She could see the resemblance to Tough—brown eyes, tall with broad shoulders, same cut cheekbones, and jutting jaw—but Torque looked harder somehow. Except when his eyes landed on Cassidy or their children. His hands, brown and dark, were gentle as he wrapped them around one of his twins when she ran ahead and lifted her to his shoulder.

She reached the group.

"Hi," Harris said. She was every librarian stereotype and never said much in public. Tough and Harris were similar in a lot of ways.

Cassidy bent to pick up a twin, and Kelly saw a smaller, bleached blond, curvy woman. "Dusty, how have you been?" Kelly asked, hurrying over to her and giving her a hug.

"Dusty just won her last motocross race. She beat the other thirty-three racers." Cassidy handed the twin her sippy cup. "All men."

"Wow." Kelly kept her arm wrapped around Dusty. "I always knew you could do it." She'd been racing for years.

"It's fun," Dusty said with a devil-may-care grin. "It's great when you get paid to do what you love."

Kelly nodded. If she married Preston, she'd continue to get paid to do more of what she loved. When did she start thinking "if"? *When* she married Preston.

"And I don't think you've met Colton, either. He's over there beside Turbo, Torque's brother." Cassidy waved toward the serious guy in the glasses.

That was three men and four women. Were they still expecting someone? She wanted to ask but didn't want to be obvious. Also, Cassidy had enough on her hands as one of the twins demanded a drink and in the next breath said she was hungry and had to pee.

"I'll take her to the restroom," Kelly said.

Cassidy sighed in relief. "Thank you so much. We've kept things as simple as we can, but this is still so much harder than I thought. Torque said we should just say our vows in front of a minister and one witness. I should have listened."

"Did I just hear 'you were right, hon?'" Torque's teeth flashed white in his dark face, and Kelly wondered if that's how Tough would look if he ever smiled.

"You did. A thousand times you did," Cassidy said.

"She's been reading Dr. T." Dusty winked.

"I thought that column was just for men?" Torque asked with a lifted brow, which clearly said he'd been handed a column or two in his time.

"There are gems in there for the ladies, too. Dr. T knows both genders equally well." Dusty grinned with a sassy shake to her head. She didn't have the refined carriage of Cassidy or the reserved personality of Harris. A blue-collar girl. *Perfect for Tough*. Kelly wasn't usually a matchmaker. Plus, the thought of Tough with someone affected her the same way nails down a chalkboard did.

"I see." Torque winked at Cassidy, who smiled, a wide smile that lit up her whole face.

Kelly lifted the twin from Cassidy's arm. "This is Nessa, right?"

Cassidy nodded. "I'm impressed! So many people can't tell them apart."

Kelly turned and started toward the back of the church, where the steps led down to the basement and, she assumed, the bathrooms. They descended down into the cool, dark interior, Nessa clinging to her neck.

"I'll try to find a light switch," she promised as they reached the bottom. She fumbled for the doorknob, finally finding it and twisting. The switches were right beside the doorway, brightening up a large fellowship hall, and the bathrooms were clearly marked down the hall to the left. She breathed deeply of the slightly musty scent tinged with stale coffee—the smell of generations of churchgoers having potlucks and spaghetti dinners, feeding the homeless and raising money for missionaries. Kelly could relate and enjoyed thinking of those earlier, unsung philanthropists.

Nessa was soon done, and after helping her wash and dry her hands, Kelly led her out of the restroom. Across the hall, beside the basement door, an old, feeble lady bent over, one hand on a cane, the other on Tough's arm.

Kelly stopped so fast, Nessa lifted her head from her shoulder to see what the problem was. Her heart stuck in her throat. She wasn't usually lacking words, but none came mind.

He leaned over, his biceps flexing as he helped the lady move her cane around a chair. His large, rough hand seemed huge compared to the frail hands of the old lady. Still in t-shirt and jeans. Clean. And boots. Cowboy boots. Her heart somersaulted backward and floated down in a cloud of stunned admiration. Tough rocked the boots. Nessa shifted in her arms, breaking her stare. "Who that?"

Tough's head jerked up. Their eyes met. Sparks seemed to fly in the hallowed basement. Unprepared for the intensity of her feelings or his gaze, Kelly gasped. Tough's brows rose, and he jerked his eyes around, as though looking for the source of her distress. *It's you.*

TOUGH'S WHOLE BODY BUZZED, like he'd barely avoided a lightning strike. Kelly did that to him, every time. But she sounded distressed, so he looked around. Was there a snake? That's what her expression said. But she wasn't looking at the ground, she was staring straight...at him.

Had he done anything to cause her to look at him like that? He didn't think so.

"I need to go to the little girls' room," Gram said.

Uh. Maybe his face registered his horror, because Kelly spoke up. "It's over here. I can...help. If you need it."

Gram lifted her head and seemed to see Kelly for the first time. She wore a tight blue skirt today—no gobs of material to hide fish fins—and a yellow and blue top with lots of ruffle things on it. A gold chain hung around her neck, a pretty contrast against her pale skin. He'd bet the metal was warm from her heat, and he'd love to kiss her, right there at the base of her neck, where it curved into her shoulder. Where the yellow gold lay. Metal on satin. He would move his lips along that contrast...

"Tough? What's wrong with you?" Gram tapped him lightly on the arm. He swallowed and pulled his eyes away from the graceful curve of Kelly's neck. She was spoken for. By someone else. Why couldn't he remember that?

"Sorry," he mumbled.

"Help me over." She tugged on his arm before she pointed her cane at Kelly. "Since I twisted this darn hip, I'll need help getting down and back up. My grandson can watch the little girl...is that Nessa?"

"Grammy." Nessa struggled to get down then toddled over to Tough and his gram.

Tough scooped her up, and she laughed. He ducked her upside down, carefully cradling her neck and back to keep his grip secure. She screamed with laughter. He'd always had trouble talking to women, but children had always been easy, and they seemed to love him.

"Uncle Tough, more!" Her warm arms circled his neck. A sharp longing clinched in his chest, which was strange. He loved children but had never had the desire for his own before. He couldn't look at Kelly, who was surely responsible for his sudden interest in procreating. He needed to get over it, get over her.

He tickled Nessa's stomach and tried to ignore the ache spiraling through his chest.

# Chapter Eight

Kelly looked away. She had to. Because she had no business admiring another man quite the way she admired Tough. Everything he did. Heck, all he had to do was stand there in his cowboy boots and she admired him. She and Preston might not be the most lovey-dovey couple ever, but she owed him fidelity.

Gram thumped her cane on the ground as she closed the distance between them, her bright orange dress contrasted with her snow-white hair, which had been curled and stuck out in a happy cloud around her head. Still, her hazel eyes brooked no nonsense. Kelly plastered her biggest, brightest smile on her face. If anyone could see through her skull into her brain and guess at her thoughts about Tough, this woman would be the one.

She offered her arm, and the old lady took it without saying anything. Good. Fooled her. For now.

They navigated the narrow hall, the coffee smell fading and the mildew scent growing stronger. One bare lightbulb lit the short passageway, and Kelly studied the gray carpet to make sure Gram didn't encounter any unexpected rolls or humps. They entered the small bathroom, and the door shut behind them before Gram spoke. "Nice ring." She indicated the large diamond engagement ring on Kelly's left hand. "Where's he at?"

"Uh." Oh, goodness. Sometimes the elderly were way too blunt. "My fiancé is heading to Southeast Asia right now."

"He's leaving you to do the wedding alone?" The woman turned and set her cane to one side, next to the pedestal sink.

"He didn't want to...I mean, I don't think he really wanted to..." Kelly maneuvered around to keep from knocking the small pot of flowers off a little table. She couldn't quite bring herself to say that she loved Preston. She didn't want to examine why that was so hard.

"Your man has money?"

"Well, yes..."

The old lady shook her head. "Can't buy something as valuable as a strong man with character."

Kelly focused on the pink floral wall border next to the ceiling. "It's not that. It's just that I have a lot of people who are depending on me to help them." She thought of Jasmine, who had spent the last two weeks shadowing Kelly after school. Clinging to the only thing in her world that wasn't shifting as her mother had announced they were moving out of their duplex and into a smaller, cheaper apartment.

Kelly helped Gram to stand. Gram shook her head. "That might be good. I understand. We all wish we had more so we could help more. Who doesn't? Maybe if you didn't have the opportunity for a better man, that Preston fellow would be enough."

Kelly shook her head. What was Gram talking about? She stiffened her spine. "He's going to be enough. Lust, or what passes for love, doesn't last anyway." There, she said it out loud. She'd never seen it last. It felt like a fairy tale. There were so many children like Jasmine. So much pain. So many eyes that cried.

"It grows deeper and gets better. But you'll never find out." Gram hobbled to the door, and they walked out.

They moved slowly down the hall. Nessa had her arms wrapped tightly around Tough's neck, and her dark head lay on Tough's shoulder, so Kelly kept a hold of Gram, while Tough held the door to the stairs and the sanctuary for them. When they reached the top, several others had been added to the group, and a lady in a pink blouse sat on the organ bench. Kelly looked at the huge pipes that lined the back wall, and a thrill went straight to her soul. No sound was closer to heaven in this world than live organ music.

"You okay?" Gram asked from beside her.

Kelly tilted her head and soaked in the sound. "I just love the organ."

"You play?"

"Oh, no. I just listen." With rapture.

"Humph." Gram's cane thumped on the step, and she slowly pulled herself up. Kelly leveraged her arm with both hands. "That's the only thing that would put Tough to sleep when he was a baby. I had a tape of Bach's organ music. He went to sleep to it for the first three years of his life."

Kelly blinked. Tough just didn't seem like a classical music kind of guy. She peeked at him from under her lashes. Cassidy had taken Nessa from him and was pointing and talking in his ear. He moved to where Cassidy directed him beside Dusty. Harris looked as uncomfortable as Colton as they stood side by side. That left the other brother, Turbo, for her. She tried to tell herself she was not disappointed.

She stepped up and introduced herself.

Turbo was shorter than his two brothers but wider, with a deeper chest. And a devilish glint in his eyes. He pumped her hand up and down. "So glad to meet you. I'll need your help later."

"Really?" She wondered what in the world for, but the pastor cleared his throat and called everyone to attention.

After they had practiced walking up the aisle and been instructed on the order of service, the pastor's attention turned to the children and their roles in the procession. Turbo tugged on her arm. "Come on."

She debated about two seconds before she followed him. He was a softer, happier version of Tough, and she was curious. What was he doing?

They slipped through the vestibule where Turbo bent and picked up a big box Kelly hadn't noticed when she walked in. He walked out and stopped on the sidewalk.

"What?" Kelly asked.

"Just wait." He put a finger up and cocked his head to the side, as though listening.

"Dude, over here. Ya think I parked it in front?" Tough's voice came up from the side of the church.

"I was waiting for you, you idiot."

"Like I would go out the same door as you. Everyone already thinks..." His voice trailed off.

Turbo smirked. "That you're chasing Kelly. Yep." His smirk got bigger. "Let 'em talk. We all know Kelly's after me." Kelly rolled her eyes as Turbo started around the side of the church. "Come on. We need to hurry."

Tough waited behind the church, standing beside an antique-looking car that was polished and shining.

"Wow. Nice car." Kelly whistled.

"Torque fixed it up for Cassidy. It was her grandfather's."

"That's sweet."

Tough had a long metal thing, and he was...

"You're going to ruin the paint? No!" Kelly shouted in a whisper.

"Relax," Turbo said. "That's a Slim Jim. Tough's unlocking the car."

"Go get the cereal," Tough said.

"I'll be right back." Turbo jogged away.

"Where's Dusty?" Kelly asked. How did Tough get away from her? They'd been sitting on the front pew together when she left.

"She's the lookout." The door clicked, and he opened it with the handle.

"Oh."

"Figure we have about ten minutes, tops." He knelt and put his upper body where the driver's legs go. "Shoot. Hand me my tools, please."

Kelly grabbed the small bag on the ground and set it on the driver's seat. "So this is why you came in the basement door. And you drove Torque's car?"

"Yeah. Can't fit all the kids in here." He pulled a metal tool with a plastic handle out of the bag then twisted his shoulders to get more deeply under the dash. "It's why we were late, too."

"The car is slow?"

He laughed. "No, ma'am. I've buried the speedometer, which maxes out at 130. Don't tell Torque."

Kelly was aghast. Not just that he was actually talking to her, but that he'd drive that fast. "With your gram in the car?"

"No." He snorted. "I had to take it back to the shop and put a clamp on the underside of the frame rail. I think there's enough room to attach that train horn."

That's when Kelly finally realized what they were doing. "You're pranking his car."

"Yep."

She looked up. "Here comes Turbo." He was using some kind of little thing with wheels to pull a big skid from the church shed. This wasn't a prank they thought of ten minutes ago.

"That's great," Tough said. "I'm almost done in here."

Turbo pulled a skid of cereal to a stop beside the car.

"I left the sunroof open," Tough said as he slid out of the front seat. He placed his tools back in the bag and shut the door before he dug a length of wire out.

"Great." Turbo grinned at Kelly. "Tough stuck this skid of cereal and the pallet dolly in the church's shed the day before yesterday."

Kelly laughed. "And you're going to pour the cereal down the sunroof?"

"No, you are. I'm headed back inside. Hey," he said to Tough who had lain down on the ground and was reaching under the car. "Gram's going to kill you if you get yourself all dirty."

"I brought a change of clothes. Depends on how much time we have."

Turbo shoved some open boxes of cereal toward her. He picked a cement block that lay in the grass and tossed it to the side, out of their way.

"Hey, watch it. You almost hit me with that."

"Relax, bro. The pain goes away eventually." Turbo turned to Kelly. "You need to get that cereal in there fast." He stopped for a minute, and his fingers touched her arm. The smile fell from his face. "I never got to ask you if this was okay?"

"It's a fun prank. I'm fine with it."

"Well, I really meant, you and Tough out here together. Tomorrow, everyone will know what you were really doing, but today..." He paused. "Today, I kinda figured that everyone will think you two were sneaking around together." Turbo grinned and nodded at Tough. "I tried to get him to do this with Dusty, but I think he's scared of her."

"You're an idiot," Tough said from under the dash.

"Oh." Kelly paused with the open box of cereal over the sunroof. Turbo reached up and dumped it in.

"That's what they make shop vacs for. Trust me." He grinned. "You're good?"

She thought of Preston and if he were to do something like this to her. Would she be okay with him allowing his name to be linked to some other woman? *As long as it wasn't true.*

"Yes." She dumped the cereal in and grabbed another box.

"You good, bro?"

"Peachy." Tough's voice was muffled since his head and shoulders were under the car. "This would have been a lot easier if I could have put it on the lift."

"Quit complaining. Kelly doesn't want to hear it." Turbo threw one last smirk over his shoulder before he sauntered off.

"Bet he was a firecracker when he was a kid." Kelly ripped open another box of cereal.

Tough snorted. "He'd come in the front door with one girl and walk out the back with another."

Kelly laughed at the picture, even though she felt bad for the girls.

A clang of metal on metal came from under the car. "I've not met the woman he couldn't charm."

"He's funny, but I'm not charmed."

Tough grunted. "He wasn't trying."

That was fair. He probably wasn't trying. And he did get her to stay with Tough even though she had a fiancé. Maybe she did get charmed.

"Could you hand me the horn?"

"Sure." Turbo had unboxed it, and she handed it to Tough before going back and opening cereal boxes as fast as she could. The floor of the car was actually getting full.

Kelly eyed the pallet. "Bet all this cereal cost a fortune."

"Turbo got Becky down at the box store to save the boxes that were out of date. That's just what she was able to keep."

"Oh. So, what's happening with the horn?"

"It'll blow every time he hits the brakes." Tough wiggled and twisted out from under the car. Kelly dumped another box in.

Tough's shoulders bunched as he pushed off the ground. "That's the plan, anyway. It's not a real train horn. There's no air compressor, and there's just not enough room, not enough time." He pulled his phone out of his pocket and looked at it. "Crap."

He dropped his tools into the bag and grabbed a cereal box. "Turbo said to hurry. Torque is getting suspicious."

Kelly tried to make her hands go faster, and they tore through the boxes in record time.

The car was almost full, and there was still a layer of boxes left when Tough's phone buzzed again. He dumped the box he was holding before reaching for the phone. He blew out a breath and shoved the phone back in his pocket. "I'm not going to have time to change. I think Torque's coming to look for us."

"Which door is he coming out?" Kelly pulled the pins and band out of her hair and shook it with her fingers. Suddenly, nothing was more important than making sure that Tough and Turbo's prank wasn't discovered. If she were jumping in, she was jumping in the whole way.

Tough glanced at his phone again, pushing cereal down with one hand and dumping a last box in. "He's headed downstairs, Turbo's trying to stall him...so probably the basement door where Gram and I came in."

She grabbed his hand. "Come on." They started running toward the door.

"Wasn't there a window at ground level right by the door?" she asked as they careened around the corner.

"I think so...yeah." Tough answered as they reached the stoop. Kelly ran into him. He tried to jerk out of her way, but his boot caught on the stoop, and they tumbled down.

She landed on top of him. His breath whooshed out beside her ear.

This wasn't exactly what she had planned, but it would look awful if they scrambled up now. They'd just have to work with it.

"I'm sorry," she whispered. She could hardly struggle to get up.

Thankfully there was only a narrow alley between the church and the next house, which looked to be a funeral parlor. They weren't in plain sight of anyone unless they were looking out the church window.

Her hair fell around them, shielding their faces as they panted, their breath mingling together. Under her, Tough was solid and hot.

He just lay there, gulping deep breaths of air. "Dang Turbo, anyway," Tough said, his gravelly voice sending pricks of current through her body.

"I'm sorry," she said, trying to move.

"No! It's not you." He reached for her, but she struggled off him, landing on her side, their legs tangled together as he moved with her, lying on his side facing her, her hair caught around his neck, his face close to hers. "It's not you." He moved one hand through her hair, threading it through his fingers, feeling the softness drift over his callouses.

His breath was coming back to him. The closeness, and the shock of her body on his, the proximity of her lips and the neck he'd been fantasizing about earlier. All the sweeping buildup of emotions poured through his body, his lungs seized, and he couldn't get enough air; it felt like he was drowning, and he wanted to pull her closer, but all he could do was feel. It was too much, too fast, too soon. He wanted it all, all of Kelly, but not that way.

His eyes dropped to her lips again. "I want to kiss you."

Her hands tightened on the hairs on the back of his neck; her body pushed closer. He forgot the reasons why he shouldn't pull her closer, forgot his very name. But she didn't say the word that would make it okay.

He touched his lips to her forehead, just above her left eyebrow. Another beside it. Just a light, feathered touch, to feel the softness, smell the freshness, taste the sweetness. Each kiss brought him closer until he touched the tip of his tongue to the necklace that lay in the curve of her neck. Hard metal. Soft, sweet skin. Warm. Just like he'd known it would be.

He lifted his head, just a little. "Kiss me, Kelly."

Conflict raged across her face, and his heart shuddered. *Choose me. Choose me.* He touched his lips to the corner of her mouth, just barely to the side. "Please."

The church door burst open. "Tough?"

Tough dropped his forehead onto Kelly's. He'd forgotten all about Torque. Well, their little play should have been convincing because it had been very real. At least on his end. He wasn't so sure about Kelly. He didn't exactly have tons of experience in kissing girls. He didn't think she was struggling to get away, but that might have been because she was pretending. There weren't too many times in his life where he wanted to punch something, but this was definitely one of them.

He hadn't been pretending. She had to know it. Now he had to face his brother.

"Really, Tough?" Torque stood in the open doorway, holding onto the doorknob, one hand on the doorframe. "Knowing Turbo the way I do, I was sure he'd dragged you and Kelly into some kind of prank." He shook his head in disbelief. "I thought she had a fiancé?" He turned to go back in. "Never mind. None of my business. You want to practice your moves some other time?" He took a step then stopped. "Sorry about that, Kelly. Nothing wrong with you at all. He's bigger, stronger, and if he had the sense God gave a goat, he'd treat you with a little class."

Turbo stuck his head out the door, under Torque's arm. "Technically, billy goats do have a certain reputation…"

"Shut up and get back upstairs." Torque shoved Turbo's head back inside.

"Come on, Tough," he said over his shoulder.

"It wasn't him…" Kelly started to say.

Tough put a finger over her lips. He wanted to quiet them another way, but…

"I'm sorry, Torque. You're right. We'll be right in," he said.

He waited until the door shut before he took his finger off Kelly's lips. Looking up, he met Torque's eyes through the glass as he walked back through the fellowship hall and to the door.

"You didn't have to lie here and take that," Kelly said softly. "I mean, I know we kind of wanted Torque to get the wrong idea so he wouldn't be suspicious of the real reason, but we hadn't meant to trip."

Or for it to be so real.

She hadn't forced him to kiss her. He'd wanted to. And more. He'd completely forgotten about fooling anyone and had been only focused on the woman beside him. Who was engaged to another man and didn't want him. But he'd forgotten. Yeah. He deserved everyone to think he was a jerk. Because he was.

"I'm sorry," he said and climbed to his feet, offering a hand down to Kelly.

"Sorry for what?" she asked. Lines appeared on her forehead. He knew how soft that skin was. Her lips turned down.

He shrugged and turned, opening the door.

"Tough." Her tone held irritation and impatience.

He turned, looking over her shoulder.

"Are we here again? Back at this spot where you won't look me in the eye and won't talk to me? Really?" She huffed then brushed past him, sweeping inside, grass still stuck to her blouse and skirt.

"Stop." He couldn't let her go upstairs like that.

She kept walking.

"Stop." He put a little more command behind it.

She ignored him. He moved after her, feeling like he was chasing her but knowing she couldn't go upstairs with grass all over her. He'd figured people might suspect something then find out tomorrow that they'd been pranking Torque's car. He had never meant for it to become something that people *knew*. He didn't want to hurt Kelly, and as much as he didn't want her to marry Preston, he didn't want to be the cause of their breakup, either.

She reached the door and yanked. He slapped his hand flat against it. The door didn't budge.

Sighing, she turned toward him. "What?"

He propped his boot against the door, so he could remove his hand. She'd said he wouldn't look her in the eye. It was true, he struggled with the intimacy of eye contact. But she wanted it, apparently. Got upset when he gave in and didn't force himself to be uncomfortable. So, deliberately, he captured her gaze with his. Tightness shifted down his jaw, but he kept his eyes on hers. His head automatically moved as though to look at the side, but he didn't lose her gaze.

Lifting his hand, he languidly moved it through the air, resting it on the back of her shoulder. She closed her eyes.

"No."

She was forcing him to look at her. She'd better keep her eyes open too.

They popped back open. He slid his hand down her slender back, down to the outward flare of her hip, catching the grass in his fingers, keeping his eyes locked with hers while his hand moved slowly. His throat burned, and his heart raced, but he refused to look away. This is what she wanted. He brought his hand around and held it up, showing her the stems he'd pulled off. Her eyes shifted, widened.

Now, he needed to talk.

His voice sounded scratchy, like it was being pulled from the very bottoms of his feet. "You have grass."

She dropped her gaze to his hand. Her lips flattened. "Thanks."

"I'd tell you to turn around so I can get it all, but I won't be able to look in your eyes."

She turned. He picked a few more blades from her blouse.

"There's more. Lower."

Her hand moved around, and he allowed himself to close his eyes, to rest from the depth of emotion. A little relief from the sweet pain that pumped with each beat of his heart. *She's not yours. She didn't choose you.*

"Did I get it all?" she asked.

He forced his eyes open. "One more."

"Where?" Her hand came around. His temple throbbed. This was torture. Devised by Romans, this was most definitely how they tortured their victims.

"Other side."

She laughed. "Okay. Got it, I think."

He took a peek. "It's gone."

"Your eyes are closed."

He opened them and stared straight into hers. *Please don't ask me to talk, too.*

She searched his gaze as though looking for something. "Ready?"

For answer, he opened the door, allowing her to walk through first, wishing he could turn and walk right out the basement door. He'd rather take Torque's car apart piece by piece in six feet of snow with crocodiles chained to both ankles than spend any more time with Kelly. Outside, she might have been pretending it was real, but now, all his energy had to be focused on pretending it wasn't.

# Chapter Nine

Kelly tramped back up the stairs. Her whole body still tingled and buzzed from Tough's touch. The first, very first thing she was going to do when she got home was call Preston. It was tacky to break off an engagement over the phone, but for the first time in her life, she was going to be tacky.

His mother would be so disappointed in her. How would Kelly break the news to her?

It didn't matter.

She had to. Surely Mrs. Fitzsimmons would understand she couldn't be rolling around on the ground, enjoying it, with another man while she was engaged to Preston. That was wrong. It was one thing to help the guys with their wedding pranks, but it was a completely different animal to do what she'd done, to feel what she'd felt. Even if things never worked out with Tough—and how could they, as different as they were—she couldn't stay with Preston now.

She stopped at the top of the steps. What was she going to do? Without Preston, her whole life plan had just evaporated. She might not have been all in with their engagement, but it wasn't like it was a surprise. Everyone, including herself, had expected it to happen sometime.

Tough put a hand on her shoulder. She realized that everyone had stopped what they were doing and stared at them. Well, Tough wasn't going to say anything, not in front of all these people, so she supposed that was up to her...

"I'm sorry we held you up." Tough's voice shocked her.

"It's okay." Cassidy smiled. "We've finished with the children, and their nanny has taken them to the park for a while." She indicated the other couples. "We've decided to pair you two together, since everyone else has been practicing. You'll be last."

While they were told where to stand and what music would be playing and how her hand would rest on his arm, Kelly tried to gather her scattered wits. Things had gotten out of hand today. She had no choice but to tell her fiancé. Before she could do that, she had to pretend she wasn't as affected as she really was, while still having Torque believe that she was so smitten with Tough that she'd lie on the grass outside and make out with him. Ugh. Too complicated.

She forced her face, which felt like an unwieldy piece of furniture attached to her neck, into a smile she hoped looked not too bright but bright enough, then she slipped her hand in the crook of Tough's elbow. Which was a mistake.

His bicep twitched, and she fought not to slide her hand up farther. Something rough scraped her palm. "Oh, you have dirt on here."

He jerked away like her touch was hot. "I'm sorry. I didn't realize."

Now that she looked a little closer, he had grass all over him. They'd been so busy brushing her off, they'd forgotten about him.

"It's everywhere." She tried to slip her hand back in, but he moved away.

"No. I don't want you to get dirty."

"It's fine. It's just grass and soil."

"No, you're clean."

Was that really the problem? Or did he not want to touch her? She tried to meet his eyes. He realized she was looking at him and started to do the eye-forcing thing he'd done downstairs, where he looked like a martyr being burned at the stake and refusing to scream as the fire licked up his legs and torso as he met her eyes.

"I just had dirt and grass all over me. We were lying on the ground, remember? I don't turn purple and die of rabies if I touch dirt."

His lips twitched. "Purple?"

"You are trying to see if I can make steam come out of my ears, aren't you?"

He closed his eyes. "It's you who's torturing me."

Her touch was torture? That bad? "You don't want me to touch you?" she asked, aghast. She pushed the hurt, surprisingly strong, aside. "Fine, but you tell Cassidy."

"No. Take my arm. They're waiting. We can do this."

"Today, if possible," Torque said from the front of the church.

"I'd say they're doomed from the start if they can't manage to get themselves down the aisle of the church without arguing about it." Dusty shifted impatiently next to Turbo, who had his hands in his pockets and a smirky little grin on his face like watching his big brother make a total and complete idiot out of her was the best entertainment he'd had in years. Kelly stifled the urge to tell him he needed to get out some. Probably his gram kept him in a cage. It was the only safe place for a guy like Turbo. If it weren't for him, they wouldn't be in this mess...

They started up the aisle. "Do you think Turbo did that on purpose?"

"Probably. Don't really know what you're talking about, but Turbo is usually guilty."

She'd been talking about Turbo allowing them to be found by Torque, but she didn't say that, because Turbo hadn't been the one to come up with the compromising position.

That had been her. An accident.

The organist was playing, and normally she loved organ music, but it was so slow. It felt like they'd never get to the end. She needed a distraction to pass the time. "Hey, don't you have another brother?"

Tough nodded. "One more. No one knows where he is."

"Oh."

"Actually, I'm not even sure he is our brother. He has a normal name," Tough said, this time out of the side of his mouth just before they parted at the top.

The rest of the rehearsal went by quickly, and less than an hour later, they were packed up and ready to go eat.

"Do you think you can find the pavilion okay?" Cassidy asked as she walked out of the church with Kelly, while Torque followed with the men and Jamal.

"It's number three, right?" Kelly asked.

Cassidy nodded, grabbing her phone and reading a text.

As they stepped out the church door, Turbo pulled out of the parking lot in his pickup. Gram's white head bounced beside him in the passenger seat. Kelly watched in confusion as Turbo grinned and waved. Hadn't Tough brought Gram? How was Tough supposed to get to the rehearsal dinner, which was going to be more like a picnic since they were holding it at the park?

When they'd been outside, Tough had mentioned he was riding with Turbo since the car he'd driven was full of cereal.

Dusty laughed from behind her. "Tough, looks like you'll have to ride with me. Turbo just took off."

Kelly turned, meeting Tough's eyes.

He didn't say anything, and neither did she. If he wanted to ride with Dusty, Kelly wasn't going to argue with him.

"Here, Tough." Dusty bumped his arm with her shoulder and handed him a helmet. "I'll even let you drive."

With one last look at Kelly, Tough turned away, still not speaking.

Kelly was just ducking into her car when a rumbling noise made her turn and look. Tough drove Dusty's bike with Dusty crouched behind him. His face was hidden behind the dark helmet, but the rest of him couldn't look any better in his tight tee, jeans, and those stinking cowboy boots, which gave her heart a thrill every time she looked at them. Dusty had her hands wrapped around his broad shoulders. Kelly told herself that the nasty, wicked feeling that ripped through her was not jealousy, but she was lying, and she knew it.

She fingered the rock on her third finger. It should come off. She needed to tell Preston.

Swallowing the acid that burned up her throat, she turned back to her car and got in.

They pulled out, but she lost them immediately in traffic. However, when she arrived at the park, they weren't there. The nasty feeling, the one she'd never felt before in her life, but which had become common fare in the last thirty minutes, pulled tight across her chest. She hopped out of her car and went immediately to where the nanny, Catherine, was trying to ride herd on the kids.

"Let me help."

Catherine, as capable as she was, gave her a grateful look. "Jamal wanted to fish in the reservoir, but I didn't want the twins that close to the water."

Kelly looked over at the sparkling water of the reservoir.

"That's great. I'll take Jamal over."

Jamal eagerly ran to where he'd laid his rod and tackle box, gathering them up and running ahead to the reservoir. Kelly followed more sedately but was grateful she had a valid excuse to avoid the stares and questioning glances. First Tough was making out with her, then he's off riding with Dusty on her motorcycle. Everyone had to wonder what was going on, what had happened. Kelly had to admit she had no idea.

It would have been one thing for Tough to ride with Dusty, but for them to be out cruising together...she couldn't think of it. Finding a bench, she was going to sit down, but Jamal came over.

"I have an extra rod. You can use it if you want."

"I've never fished before." Although someone had recently asked her if she had fins. She almost smiled at the memory before she remembered that the person who had asked that was now cruising around with another woman.

"Really? Never?"

"Nope."

"Here, take this." He handed her a small, round container.

"What's this?"

"Worms."

Kelly blinked. She held the container a little farther from her body. "Do they bite?"

Jamal's eyes drew down. "I don't think so. I don't think they have teeth." He took the container from her and opened the lid. Kelly took another small step backward. Her knees hit the edge of the bench. Jamal waved the container around. "You have to dig in and grab a worm. Then we put him on the hook, and that's what brings the fish."

Kelly put her best appease-the-child face on and tried not to let on that she didn't want to touch the worms. "Could you show me once, first?"

"Sure." Jamal smiled and puffed out his chest. Kelly grinned to herself. Lots of people enjoy fishing. It was probably fun. Once one got past the worm part.

~

BY THE TIME Tough finally pulled Dusty's bike into the park and shut it off at the pavilion they'd rented, everyone was sitting down, eating.

"They have drinks," he said as he took his helmet off. Dusty said she'd promised to bring tea, so they'd gone across town to the only store that carried the kind of tea she wanted. Tough suspected something wasn't ringing quite true, and he wanted to blame Turbo, but for once, Turbo looked extremely uncomfortable, having somehow gotten stuck in a corner beside the red-haired librarian...Harris, he thought her name was.

"It was a nice ride." Dusty smiled at him and blinked her eyes. Was she flirting? He really wasn't used to all this talking and being around people. He supposed he had Kelly to thank for it. She'd forced him to make eye contact...no, he'd forced himself. Just like he'd forced himself to talk to her. He was glad he had. Not so glad he couldn't get his mouth to work earlier when Dusty suggested he ride with her. He'd wanted to go with Kelly. But she hadn't spoken up, and his tongue might be getting better at moving when it was supposed to, but it hadn't done it then.

He grunted at Dusty and grabbed the gallons of tea from her saddlebag. He scanned the pavilion again. Where was Kelly? Her car was in the lot.

Cassidy walked over to him, her plate filled with jello, mac and cheese, and other foods for the twins. "She's fishing with Jamal."

Tough jerked his head. "Thanks," he mumbled, not even wanting to know how Cassidy knew he was looking for Kelly.

"Hey, no problem. Why don't you go tell them that we're eating? I think they probably know, but it might remind Jamal that he's hungry."

He nodded, turning and striding toward the reservoir, which wasn't far away, just around the bend. Sure enough, Kelly stood along the edge, in her yellow shirt and blue skirt, holding a fishing pole.

The end of it tipped down. She didn't seem to notice that she had something on the line. But Jamal yelled, jumping up and down. She jerked then started to wind the line in as he encouraged her. Whatever she had, it looked heavy.

She got the fish to shore, just as Tough reached her. In all the excitement, he didn't think she'd noticed him. Or maybe she was deliberately ignoring him. At any rate, he looked around for a net and didn't see one.

"What is it?" Jamal asked.

"I'm not sure," Tough said. "It kind of looks like a big goldfish."

Kelly gasped at the sound of his voice and jerked the rod up as she turned. She hadn't been ignoring him, apparently. The fish, which had been flopping on the ground, jerked in the air when she lifted the rod.

"I wouldn't..." Tough reached out to grab the line, intending to pull the fish back on the ground so it didn't slip off the hook, but he was too late.

The fish fell off. The hook jerked back from the released tension. He lurched to cover Kelly.

She squealed. "Ouch."

Had he hurt her? He backed away. A red spot began on her shoulder. Just a pinprick at first. But then it grew bigger. Shiny, thin metal poked out. The hook had embedded in her shoulder. So deep he couldn't see anything but a small flash of metal and the fishing line coming out of her blouse.

He pulled the lighter out of his pocket and burnt the line, disconnecting her from the fishing rod, at least.

He looked around. Jamal had thrown the fish back into the pond, and now he stood beside him, staring at Kelly. "It's in her shoulder, isn't it?" Jamal said. "That's why she's bleeding." The boy looked a little green and glanced away. "Hey, something has my line!" Jamal shouted, and he ran off.

"Say something, Kelly." It bothered him how she just stood there.

She grimaced. "I'm afraid if I move, it will hurt."

"They're not going to bring the hospital to you."

She narrowed her eyes at him. "This is a great time for you to find both your tongue and your sense of humor."

"Sorry. What do you want me to say? You're going to die?"

Her eyes flew open wide, and she affected a simper. "Oh, my gosh. Do you really think so?"

His lips twitched. "No."

Her eyes narrowed again. "Hauling girls around on motorcycles must really make you happy. That's two jokes in less than a minute."

"Girls have never made me happy." They still didn't. There was just one. There had always been just one.

"This is not the time to step out of the closet."

One side of Tough's mouth hitched up. "Now *you're* making jokes. I wish you'd take this seriously. You're going to stand here and bleed to death."

She smiled. Then her face melted into a worried frown. "Do you really think I need to go to the hospital?"

He paused. "Can I look?"

"Of course."

"Well...you're probably going to have to unbutton your shirt. Maybe just two buttons."

"I'm sure I can trust you to be the perfect gentleman."

She must have forgotten how much trouble he had being the perfect gentleman while they were lying on the ground and he was begging to kiss her.

He didn't answer her. But, as she unbuttoned her shirt, he slid it over until the hook was visible. Actually, just the end of the hook was visible.

"How bad is it?" She turned her head, almost bumping his cheek with her nose.

He took a breath.

"That bad?"

"Well, the thing is, with fishhooks, they have those little barbs on them, to keep from losing the fish. Which means you can't really pull it backward. You kind of have to push it through."

"And you can do that?"

"Well...no." He let go of her shirt. "I could if the other end of the hook were visible—the sharp end. But it's buried in your shoulder."

If it were him or one of his brothers, they'd take a pair of needle-nose pliers and manipulate the hook until it broke the skin, then pull it out. But he didn't want to do that with Kelly.

"So, ER?"

"I think that's best. I'll take you."

She bit her lip. "I'd appreciate that. I'd hate to ruin the meal for Cassidy."

He put an arm around her, to steady her, of course, and they started walking to the car. "The last I looked, Turbo was stuck beside Harris and looking as miserable as I've ever seen him. I hope Harris stays there all night."

Kelly chuckled. "You're mean."

"Not so. I'm sure Harris is a very nice person, but she's not buying Turbo's crap. Good for her."

# Chapter Ten

T he *EMERGENCY* sign flashed above the hospital door. Kelly waited while Tough got out and walked around the car to help her out. The ride wasn't as bad as she'd expected. Her shoulder throbbed, but there was no new sharp, unbearable pain.

Tough opened her door, and Kelly put her feet on the ground carefully, keeping her right arm from moving. Tough reached in and gently took her left, helping her to stand.

They'd chosen the smaller hospital on the edge of town over the larger one in the middle of the city, and it seemed like a good choice. There was no one in the waiting room, and the nurses took her right back. She exchanged her shirt for a hospital gown, and Tough strode in after she was decent. Decent except for the unsnapped shoulder, which exposed the bit of metal and line sticking out of the fleshy part of her shoulder.

His brows drew together, and she wanted to reassure him. "They've already given me a shot of Novocain. She said the doc would be in in about twenty minutes once it takes full effect, and they'd have it out in less than five."

He studied her shoulder before saying, "Sounds easy."

"Yeah." She fiddled with the edge of her gown. "Tough?"

"Mmm?"

Her heart thumped in her chest, and she didn't lift her eyes from staring at her hand in her lap. "I'm going to break off my engagement."

She had promised herself she wouldn't chase Tough, and she wasn't going to. But it was fair to let him know where she stood.

"Why?" He sounded truly baffled.

Her mouth worked up and down. "Why? Well, because, because I..."

A corner of his mouth lifted. "Think hard."

She laughed, shaking her head. "It's been a crazy day."

"Yeah. Don't make a rash decision." His serious expression confused her.

Was he trying to talk her out of breaking up with Preston? Sure seemed like it.

"It's not rash. I've been having some thoughts about it for a while now." Since her car crash and she met Tough for the first time as an adult.

"He can give you everything you've always wanted." The muscles in Tough's cheeks worked as he stared straight ahead. She didn't try to get him to meet her eyes. "You two could do a lot of good together if you teamed up. That's what you want. It's what you've always wanted."

He ran his hand over his head and paced to the window and back. "If you're worried about what happened earlier, you were pretending, remember?"

"Of course," she said, but it came out more like a whisper. He hadn't seemed like he was pretending when he ran his lips down her throat and nipped at her necklace. Nor when he begged her to kiss him. His "please" rang in her ears still. Had he really been pretending?

"Don't throw away the chance to do what you've always wanted to do." He looked her in the eye, then. His face was blank. There was no pretense or hidden pain. She had to assume he was sincere.

She was the one who looked away first. "I have to tell him what I did."

He nodded slowly. "I admire honesty."

She glanced up, and their eyes met again. Held. Seconds of silence ticked by as she tried to figure out if she was misunderstanding him.

The doctor bustled in, breaking the elongated silence. "Okay. Is that shoulder nice and numb?"

The nurse followed him in and arranged instruments on a tray. "You're going to want to be on this side, sir. Give her your hand. This shouldn't hurt, and we'll be done in no time, but a little distraction will help push things along."

Tough moved silently. He paused before touching her fingers. She didn't move. Not to hold his hand. Not to pull away.

He slid his hand along hers, the roughness of his callouses sending burning currents up her arm. On its own, her hand flexed and turned, their fingers twining together like they'd done it all their lives, instead of this being the first time. Her hand fit perfectly in the larger cradle of his, and her heart felt warm.

She didn't want to ruin the feeling by examining it too closely, so she closed her eyes. His thumb moved along the surface of her hand, just a gentle touch. She opened her eyes to watch. His hand dark. Hers light. His rough, hers smooth. His nails blunt and still with a little bit of black grease stuck in several. Hers pink and shiny. His wrist thick, hers much smaller with golden bracelets dangling.

So different. Yet it felt so perfect to have him holding her.

He wanted her to stay with Preston.

There was a tug on her shoulder, and the doctor moved and held up a pliers-type instrument. "It's out," he said with a smile. "I'm putting a little Neosporin on this, then you're free to go."

"No antibiotics?" Tough asked, causing Kelly to turn her head. He'd spoken. Wow.

"Nope." The doctor put a hand on her shoulder. "If you haven't had a tetanus shot, I recommend scheduling that immediately. That will be in your discharge instructions. With this being a small hospital, we don't see enough people through here, and the vaccine expires before we use it. So we don't stock it. Otherwise, I don't expect any problems. Any other questions?" he asked.

"No," Kelly said.

Tough walked out behind the doctor, and she put her shirt, which was slightly worse for wear, back on, before gathering up her stuff and walking out into the hall.

Tough leaned against the wall, his head tilted back, eyes closed. "Napping?"

He straightened. "Yeah. Been a day."

She noted the tightness around his eyes; he'd been up early and probably had little time between work and the rehearsal. She fought the urge to trace his jaw with her fingers or rub his tense shoulders. He blinked.

"It sure has. I can drop you off at the shop," Kelly offered, looking away.

He shook his head. "No. I'll see you to your car, if you're sure you can drive?"

"I can. Now that there's not a fishhook stuck in my shoulder." It was sore, but there was a feeling of relief, even if it was only mental, with having it out.

He nodded. "Well, good. I'll find my own way home." He shortened his stride to match hers.

She fingered the key and stopped. "I'm not going to just leave you here at the hospital."

"And I don't want you to drive me home." He kept walking.

"Why not?"

"I just don't."

She stopped and crossed her arms over her chest. "Your girlfriend's going to be there, and you don't want me to see her?"

"Does it matter?" he asked, stopping beside her. She glimpsed maybe a hint of bitterness or resentment in him for the first time. But he blinked, and the tightness around his eyes was gone as if she'd imagined it.

"Of course not."

He stared at the wall. Finally, he shifted. "I'll drive you home."

"No. If you don't want me to take you home, that's fine." She felt like stomping as she walked by him and out the sliding doors into the hospital foyer and waiting area.

He matched her stride. "I'm sorry."

"You're being a chauvinist." She didn't slow down, and she didn't bother looking at him.

The outside doors opened automatically, and they walked through.

She thought he wasn't going to answer her, and she told herself she didn't care.

Finally, they reached her car. Tough stopped with his hand on the handle. "No. It was pride." He rubbed the back of his neck. "I live at the shop. There's a little room behind the office. I have a bunk there. Never needed or wanted anything else. Just somehow, I knew that wouldn't sound very good to you, and I didn't..."

Shock rolled through her. He didn't have a house. Or an apartment. Nothing. He lived in his shop. In a garage. She tried to process that and just couldn't. Would he be considered...homeless?

No, surely not. But...

She waited, but he didn't move or speak. Finally, she prompted, "Didn't what?"

"Didn't want you to think less of me than you already do," he said then opened her door. "Drive carefully. Of course, you don't have to, but I'd really appreciate a text when you get home."

"You deserve one." He made to shut the door, but she held a hand up. "You live at the shop because you want to, not because you have to."

"Yes." He breathed out heavily. "But it doesn't really matter. You see what I was saying earlier? Preston can give you what you want."

She was starting to think that he was wrong. Not because Preston couldn't give her what she once wanted, but because he couldn't give her what she wanted now. Had she changed that much?

She put her hand down, and Tough shut her door. The engine fired up. Finding the button, she lowered the window. "Sure you don't want a ride?"

"I need to walk. Tomorrow is more of the same kind of torture today has been." Although she knew he was serious, there was also a small twinkle in his eye. She grinned back at that twinkle.

"Maybe for you, but I'm planning on staying away from fishhooks, and I guarantee that you won't find me lying on the ground in my bridesmaid dress."

His lips twitched. She'd almost gotten a smile out of him. Pulling the car into gear, she drove away.

～

KELLY PULLED into Cassidy's drive that evening for what would be a very tame almost-bachelorette party. Orange light glowed in the windows on the left wing of the house, although the soaring great room windows that took up most of the front middle of the mansion were dark. It was a little hard to picture Torque living here, but it was a great place for their kids, and Torque's shop was on the property, too.

Kelly pushed the heavy wooden door open and stepped inside the huge, two-story entrance. Laughter came from her left, and she started that way, admiring the polished wood, tile floors, and a small glimpse of Cassidy's huge, modern kitchen.

This is the kind of house that Preston and she would live in. No question it was nice.

Tough lived in his garage.

He would probably buy a house if he got married. Maybe? How would she know? She shook her head. Why was she even thinking about it? But she couldn't seem to get the thought out of her head. Being with Tough wouldn't mean luxury. Would it matter? Not to the woman who loved him. At least that's what her heart said.

Kelly walked into the large living room. Comfortable chairs and a large sectional couch were placed strategically around a massive stone fireplace. Cassidy squealed when she saw her and jumped up. "Kelly's here!" She ran over and gave her a hug. "So glad you could make it. Help yourself to a drink and some snacks." She waved a hand at the wet bar against the far wall where a spread fit for a small banquet was laid out.

Kelly helped herself, answering questions about the fishhook ordeal while she loaded her plate and grabbed a lemon water.

She took a seat while Dusty regaled them about a fellow driver's wedding that took place in the French Alps.

When Dusty finished, Harris's head swiveled to Kelly. Her gaze was direct. "So you and Tough? Did you break off with Preston?" The gaze of all three women went to her ring finger where Preston's ring weighed her hand down like a boat anchor.

What should she say? All her emotions were in a huge jumble, and she had no idea what she should do. Of course, what actually happened this afternoon wasn't what anyone thought.

Dusty spoke up before she could answer, "I wanted to say that I was sorry if I offended you by taking Tough on my bike. I think my heart was in the right place."

"She said something to me about her plan, and I told her to go for it, so you can blame me, too," Harris spoke up.

"What plan?" Kelly asked with a frown.

"I just thought that it was a little unfair, Tough working with a handicap like Preston. I thought maybe it would be good for you to see the shoe on the other foot." She shrugged. Her ruffled blouse exposed one tanned shoulder.

Harris leaned forward earnestly. "Yeah, I agreed. You know. See the guy you're crushing on with another woman."

She couldn't be irritated with her friends, despite the jealousy that had eaten up her insides. Dusty would have her best interests at heart. "Is it a crush?" That was hitting pretty close to the questions she'd had all her life about love. Did love really last? With who?

"You didn't tell us about Preston," Cassidy pointed out. "Did you break up?"

Kelly shrugged. "I don't know."

"You don't know if you broke it off with Preston?" Her regal eyebrow lifted.

"I can't right now. He's on an airplane, and he's flying to Southeast Asia." She sighed. "Can I break off an engagement over the phone and across three continents?"

"Yes," everyone chorused at once.

Kelly held up a carrot like it would protect her from the ganging up of her friends. "Really? I've always heard that was tacky."

"If he loved you and was going to be devastated, I'd say let's think about it. But neither of you are going to be devastated," Cassidy said from where she sat, curled up in a recliner, just a small amount of food on her plate. Probably too nervous to eat. Or excited.

Kelly rubbed the carrot back and forth in the creamy vegetable dip. "We love each other." Why did she feel so defensive? "I feel bad about Mrs. Fitzsimmons. I'm worried about her reaction." She held the carrot up. "Then, we have plans. Things we're going to do together. We've been planning this in some form since before high school graduation." Her stomach cramped and spun at the thought of stepping off that cliff.

"So, live without a plan," Dusty said with an easy grin. She sat on one leg, with the other leg crossed and her foot swinging slowly. Relaxed.

Easy for the motocross driver to say.

Cassidy seemed to think that as well because she said, "That works for you very nicely, Dusty. But some people can't live while letting go."

"Like a rollercoaster," Harris said.

"Right, some people can't let go," Kelly echoed. She didn't ride rollercoasters.

"But sometimes you just have to be convinced to get on. Once you're on, you love it and keep going back for more." Cassidy leaned over and patted Kelly's hand. "I can't force you to get on the rollercoaster, but think about it. Is it going to hurt?"

"I've got this feeling that it could." Kelly bit her lip. Was fear holding her back? Her heart shouted a resounding *yes*.

"Are you going to live your life afraid that something might hurt?" Dusty asked.

Kelly set the carrot down because she couldn't control the overwhelming need to twist her hands together.

"Um, excuse me," Harris said, "but maybe I should take the other side. I mean, people live perfectly happy lives making safe choices every day. Confronting fear is a good thing, but avoiding those things that you're afraid of can keep you safe and healthy, too." Harris was normally the most quiet when they all got together, but she kept talking. "I guess I'm saying, Kelly, that I think it's obvious that you're afraid. Leaving Preston, who's been your solid anchor for so long, exploring the idea that there might be love for you, an exciting, real love, when you've spent your whole life convincing yourself that passionate love doesn't last, and changing the whole picture of what you thought your life was going to be like. I mean, Tough seems like a great guy, but let's face it. You're not going to be doing charity galas with him. And he's not going to be dragging you around to political rallies." Harris smiled softly, her red hair glowing in the firelight. She picked her tea up and sipped. It had been a long speech for her.

"You just put into words everything that's been rattling, unorganized, around in my head. Maybe it boils down to the fact that I think I might want to leave Preston because I think I might be in love with Tough. And maybe the love I feel for Preston isn't the kind a wife should feel for her husband. But I've never thought that kind of love lasted. I've always thought it was a rather stupid way to pick a life partner. Shared goals and dreams. Compatibility. Common sense. All that seems much smarter."

"Someone from the same social construct as you?" Dusty asked softly.

She hadn't come from money. Tough had led her to it. Even tonight, he'd been basically saying that he thought she should stay with Preston because Preston could offer her things he couldn't. "Yeah. That too. Same social construct."

"So, what happens if you're wrong? What happens if passionate love really is a thing? And it lasts?" Cassidy asked thoughtfully.

"And what if for the rest of your life you dream about Tough?" Harris asked over the rim of her teacup.

"When you see him, you wish you were with him?" Dusty asked.

"What if money really doesn't buy happiness?" Harris chimed in. Although Kelly wasn't really thinking that Preston's money was key to her happiness. It was more that they were compatible. For the most part. They loved each other in a calm, rational way.

"Because you can't buy loyalty, devotion, consideration," Cassidy said.

"A man who has time for you."

"Someone who will sit on the porch and listen to the rain with you."

"Someone who loves you but will let you go if it might be better for you."

They were coming at her from all sides. "Okay, okay." Kelly held her hand up. "I get it. BUT that doesn't answer my fundamental question—will it last? I mean how many fifty-somethings do you see sitting on the porch listening to the rain together? AND, even more importantly, I don't even know if Tough likes me like that. I'm not sure what I feel either."

"Okay." Cassidy straightened on the couch. Her analytical, lawyerly face on. "You have two different things to think about. One. Do you want to stay with Preston? It would be wrong to break up with Preston, try Tough out, decide you don't want him, and go running back to Preston, right?"

Kelly nodded slowly. She didn't want to do that.

"So. Do you want to stay with Preston, giving up everything that might or might not come with finding what could be the right guy, or would you consider hurting the woman who basically raised you and expects you to marry her son, giving up all your life's plan and basically starting from nothing rebuilding your life? Whether Tough is in the picture or not." She paused, for dramatic effect, maybe. Like they were in a courtroom. "Then, if you decide yes, *then* you can think about your feelings for Tough, his for you, and what to do about it." She nodded and leaned back. "Make sense?"

Kelly thought about it for a minute. Everyone else was quiet too. Finally, she shook her head. "Mrs. Fitzsimmons is important to me. I don't want to hurt her. Tough and I might not work out. Then what? Plus, it's not just my life's plan. This is what Preston has planned forever, too. I don't want to break his heart."

Dusty shook her head no, but Cassidy nodded slowly. "I see your point," she said.

"So, when is the last time you and Preston shared a passionate kiss?" Dusty asked.

The room fell silent.

Too bad she didn't still have her carrot. She needed something to do to avoid the uncomfortable stares that faded into shock then pity.

"We don't have that kind of relationship." She felt defensive again.

"You have kissed?"

"Of course."

"And what was it like?"

Kelly looked down. It hadn't been horrible. But it wasn't like she longed to do it again. Tough hadn't kissed her, but she longed for him to.

"I see what you're saying." Kelly wiped her hands down her pants. "I mean, I'm definitely attracted to Tough, but is that enough? I just can't believe that it will be in twenty years. Won't that fade?"

"Some, I think," Cassidy admitted. "I guess I can tell you in fifty years." She grinned, and Kelly felt a little jab of guilt because she was getting married tomorrow and here Kelly was talking about how love didn't last.

"What would it take for you to change your mind?" Harris asked.

"About love? About it needing to be passionate?" Kelly asked.

"About it being enough, too. You're attracted to Tough, but don't you like him?"

"He never talks!" Kelly exclaimed, but she knew it wasn't true. The guy was funny when he did talk. And patient. Just look at all the old men in his garage. And kind. He was starting next week helping her with her renovations and wasn't going to charge a thing.

"I saw him whispering in your ear yesterday." Dusty grinned.

Kelly smiled. "Okay. I like him, I'm attracted to him, but I don't know if that's enough."

"I guess that's where the fear comes in. If you want a safe, secure life, if you don't want to rock the boat. Choose Preston. Maybe you really do love him, and we're wrong. If you want the possibility of more, with a greater likelihood of pain and disillusionment, choose Tough." Harris set her tea down and leaned back, her brows drawn together. "As for Mrs. Fitzsimmons, I know she does kind of have her heart set on you two marrying, but I think she has her heart set more on you being happy. Basically, I don't think you need to worry about her if you choose Tough."

Kelly looked down at her mostly untouched plate. "If he'd even have me."

"Oh, he'll have you," Harris said. "But I agree that shouldn't be your security blanket. If you're leaving Preston, leave. Don't have him as your backup, and don't have Tough as your landing pad."

"Right," Kelly said. "That's just consideration for them as well as myself." She was worried about hurting Preston, and it would change his world and his future as much as hers. Still, he wouldn't have a problem finding someone else. Sure, she was an automatic date anytime he needed it. Except for this trip. It was the first time she'd not been available for him. Once again, she wondered if Preston might miss the warmth of a more romantic-type relationship. Maybe he'd be relieved if she broke up with him.

"Okay, we've wasted enough time on me..."

"Wait! I know. We can write to Dr. T," Harris spoke excitedly for the first time that evening.

"He only answers men," Dusty pointed out.

"You read him?" Cassidy asked her in shock.

"Of course. Who doesn't? Plus, he claims to be a mechanic. The guys on the circuit love him." Dusty shrugged.

"It's a woman," Kelly said flatly.

"So write! Tell her you must have an answer, even if it's private! Since you can't decide for yourself, let her do it for you!" Harris bounced on her seat in her excitement, almost upsetting the plate of chips and dip in her lap.

"Live my life according to what Dr. T says?" Kelly asked, the idea going against everything she knew.

Cassidy tilted her head. "Have you ever heard anyone say she doesn't give great advice? Might as well utilize her experience and professional opinion."

"She's started doing her column every day, so maybe she'll start answering women, too. You never know," Dusty pointed out reasonably.

Why not? It wasn't like she had to do whatever the columnist said. She could still choose for herself. "Okay. I'll write her tonight when I get home."

"Why wait?" Dusty asked. "Do it now. On your phone."

"No. I want to phrase it just right." If she was going to do it, she didn't want to rush through it. Dr. T needed all the facts to make an informed decision. "Now, enough about me. Isn't someone else having any drama in their life?" She looked pointedly at Cassidy, who laughed and started talking about the wedding and honeymoon and juggling the kids through it all.

# Chapter Eleven

Getting up early so he could work on his column before getting dressed in his monkey suit, Tough sipped his coffee and sat at his computer, going through the new questions that had come in. Sometimes he really enjoyed this job. Sometimes it broke his heart, because there were just some things that couldn't be fixed. Not by him, anyway. Today was a mixed bag, and he was having trouble concentrating. After all, his big brother was getting married in a few short hours.

Tough had never thought he might do the same someday, but after spending the last few weeks with Kelly, he'd begun to long for a woman, a companion, someone to laugh with, eat with, share his day with, work with, and do something meaningful in life with. He ached to hold her, and his arms felt empty. Unfortunately, the only woman that his body and soul would accept to fill the void he hadn't even known he had was Kelly.

He had tried to picture various other women but not for long, because it didn't work. His being didn't long for their touch, their voice, their scent. He didn't admire them and want to spend hours just watching them. He couldn't picture lying on clean green grass and running his fingers through their hair.

Ugh. He reached up and shut the monitor off with a snap. He was wasting his time...wait. He turned the monitor back on. Surely, he had conjured up her name because that's what he wanted to see...surely, he'd been mistaken.

But as the monitor flashed back on, he could see that he wasn't mistaken. Kelly Irwin, Brickly Springs, PA, at the bottom of his screen. He opened the email.

*Dear Dr. T,*

*My friends and I have read and admired you for a long time. I know this is a column for men, but I'm hoping you will make an exception for me, either publicly or with a private answer. Here's my problem:*

*I have a long-standing arrangement with a man I grew up with from an affluent family. He just became my fiancé. We have a solid friendship, and I owe a huge debt to his mother, who has always hinted at how much she would love to see us married. We love each other. Of course we do. It's a win-win for both of us, especially since I do not believe in passionate love lasting. It's great for a while, but then it fades, and all you have left is basically what I have now—a good friend.*

*The problem is that I'm afraid I might be falling in love with someone else. The feelings are stronger than I ever thought they could be. I think about this person constantly and want to be with him every second. I look at him, and my heart sings. I understand poetry now and why men would risk everything they've spent their whole lives building just to be with a woman. The man I'm infatuated with is a good man. Steady. A blue-collar worker. In fact, he has integrity and character, where my fiancé has maybe just a façade, I believe.*

*From the time I was little, I saw my mom move from man to man. I'm a social worker, and I work with kids every day whose parents were passionately "in love" and now are in divorce court, while their kids come to me, crying. Heartbroken. It hurts. And I wonder because no couple goes into a marriage thinking it's not going to last, but half the time, it doesn't. How do I know that my passionate love actually will last? I am afraid to take that chance.*

*By the way, I mentioned the social status of the two men because, after some deep reflection on my part, there are two main things that make a couple "fall out of love." One is adultery, and the other is fighting about money. Is this your experience as well?*

*I don't want to give up what I have and replace it with someone I'll regret years down the road when our "love" fades. How do I know? How do I choose? What should I do? And, to be honest, I don't even know if the guy I'm falling for feels the same for me.*

*Thanks in advance for your help.*
*Kelly Irwin, Brickly Springs, PA*

Tough stared at the screen. Kelly Irwin was a pretty common name, but there could be no doubt that it was *his* Kelly. His.

He didn't even have to think about what his answer would be. But he didn't want to say it. Didn't want to write it. And wouldn't. Not today.

He shut his computer off. Today was his brother's wedding. Kelly would be there. He would enjoy it. He would spend time with Kelly. He would be a friend. He would look her in the eye. He would force his tongue to work. He would try to flirt if that were possible. He would have a good time with a nice girl, then he would come home and tell her what she needed to hear: stay with Preston. Because Tough wasn't good enough.

KELLY STOOD at the back of the church, listening to the beautiful organ music. If she continued with her wedding plans, it was definitely going to include a huge organ and a massive sanctuary to get the full acoustic effect.

So far, she'd been with the girls and hadn't seen Tough. It wasn't exactly a typical wedding because of the kids and Cassidy's and Torque's relaxed attitudes. Things had been a little chaotic.

Still, he had to be somewhere close. Not only was her skin pricking, but it was almost time for them to walk up together. She had not looked for him, and he had not stepped up beside her. She moved forward as Colton and Harris stepped out slowly together. Turbo stood at the head of the church with a glint in his eye. He had something planned, she was sure. Hopefully it wasn't something that was going to ruin Cassidy's big day.

She lifted her chin. She would walk up by herself if Tough didn't show. It wouldn't surprise her too much if he didn't anyway, as much as he hated crowds and being in front of people. A little shiver of disappointment curved around her neck. She would have bet that he would face his fear and fulfill his responsibilities.

Giving herself a mental shake, she firmly insisted it didn't matter. She hadn't gotten to talk to Preston last night. Just a few texts. She couldn't break up with him with a text. But she *had* sent the email to Dr. T.

Harris and Colton reached the halfway point.

Tough materialized beside her. Even though she was expecting him, his presence still startled her, and she jerked her head around to look at him. Which was a mistake.

He wore a tux, and he wore it better than anyone she'd ever seen in one, and she'd seen a lot of men in tuxes. The cut broadened his shoulders while the white shirt contrasted with his dark complexion. He stared down into her eyes. His own were dark, more mahogany than walnut. She shivered from the intensity and looked away.

His arm was up, waiting for her to place her hand on it. His hands had been scrubbed. Pink patches of skin and a few red scabs showed where he'd taken the skin off to get the grease out. Her heart pinched at the thought of Tough, alone in his garage, scrubbing his hands until they bled to get rid of the stains of his honest labor. Tears pricked her eyes. She blinked. She couldn't cry. Not over Tough washing his hands. What was wrong with her?

She swallowed and turned her lips up, looking again into his eyes as she slipped her hand in the cradle of his arm. Even through the fabric of his tux, his arm was solid and roped with muscle.

"You okay?" he asked in a rough whisper.

She nodded.

He jerked his head, and they started down the aisle. It wasn't her wedding, and it wasn't her day, but she had to fight to keep from closing her eyes to savor the feeling. The majestic organ music and the just man beside her were more than enough to fill her soul to overflowing with peace and contentment. She would never have this feeling with Preston. But were feelings enough to base a life on? At this moment in time, she wanted to say yes, because she never wanted this amazingness to end.

They reached the end of the aisle where they parted. Her hand felt empty and her heart alone as they separated. She wanted to hold on, to never let go. Was *this* love?

Jamal made it down the aisle without incident. The twins weren't so blessed. There were two of them but only one basket, and they both wanted to be the only one to carry it. The guests got several good laughs out of their antics before Catherine caught them and sat them down. One big lump of flower petals lay in a heap right in the middle of the aisle. They made it out of the basket, at least. She met Tough's eyes, and both corners of his mouth tilted up. Her stomach curled, low and warm.

Cassidy, the most beautiful bride Kelly had ever seen, walked sedately up the aisle, and the ceremony began. Kelly listened with half an ear until Jamal walked up the steps with the pillow on which the rings were supposed to be. One small ring nestled on the pillow, along with another huge ring that looked to be big enough to put in a bull's nose... Turbo had a big smirk on his face. Kelly rolled her eyes and glanced at Tough, wondering if he had anything to do with it. He lifted a shoulder almost imperceptibly. It wasn't him. She breathed out in relief.

Some of the guests who were closer and could see tittered, and some, probably the ones who knew Turbo and had expected something of that nature, laughed out loud. Cassidy didn't appear to be upset, which gave Kelly the freedom to enjoy.

"This ring appears to be a little big. Do we have another?" the pastor asked with a sparkle in his eye that led Kelly to believe this wasn't his first rodeo either.

Turbo reached into his lapel and pulled out a Cracker Jack box.

*Of course. It's in the box.* But the box appeared to be unopened.

"Maybe you'll find something you can use in here. After all, you always said I got my driver's license from a Cracker Jack box," Turbo said, handing the box to Torque.

Torque took the box with a long-suffering grimace and opened it. Turbo held his hands out while Torque dumped the box of popcorn into them. He easily cupped the contents of the small box of cereal in his two massive hands.

No ring. Torque's lips pinched. He turned the empty box toward him and stuck a finger in. He pulled out a small green whistle.

"That ain't gonna work," Turbo said, still smirking.

Kelly didn't turn her head, but she could hear shuffling and whispers coming from the guests seated mere feet away from them.

A muscle in Torque's cheek began to twitch.

Turbo dropped the popcorn on the floor and crossed his arms over his chest. "Give him the ring, Tough. Quit messing around. I'd like to eat today."

Everyone's face whipped to Tough. His wide eyes, raised brows, and slightly parted lips told Kelly as plain as day that he had no clue what Turbo was talking about. Still, he closed his mouth, his jaw muscles bunching together, and slowly, almost fatalistically, put his hands in his pockets. His left hand came back out, holding a bright pink ribbon to which was tied a small, shiny, golden band.

The guests clapped and cheered.

Torque grabbed it.

"Man, Tough," Turbo said. "Don't you think it's time you grew up and stopped acting like a kid everywhere you go? This isn't the time or the place..."

"Shut up," Torque growled.

Harris looked horrified. Cassidy seemed resigned. Tough's face was bright pink even over his tanned complexion. Kelly had the strangest urge to laugh.

Thankfully that was all Turbo had planned for the ceremony, although the pastor might have rushed the rest of it, because Torque and Cassidy were married shortly after. Which was just as well, since the kids were getting restless.

He presented the beaming couple, who walked down the aisle. The wedding party followed. Since the receiving line would be at the reception, they went straight out the back doors of the sanctuary.

"Come on." Tough grabbed her elbow. "You want to see if the horn thing works?"

She allowed herself to be pulled out the front door. "I thought the car was in the back?" But there it sat, down at the end of the steps and still filled to the top with cereal.

"I left it in neutral. Turbo pushed, and I steered with the rope I attached to the steering wheel."

She'd been to a lot of weddings, but she'd already had more fun at this one than at any of the others she'd been to, and they hadn't even made it to the reception. Although she had to hand it to Cassidy. She wasn't sure there was another woman on the planet who would remain unruffled by Turbo's antics.

The bridal party stood on the steps as Torque and Cassidy walked to their car.

"Nice ring, Cassidy. Don't lose the whistle, you might need it." Turbo's smirk had gotten bigger.

"So I can ram it down your throat," Torque said, but he laughed as he did so and pulled Cassidy closer to his side before leaning down and kissing her.

"If you weren't such a good babysitter, we would never put up with you," Cassidy said with a grin as they walked down the steps.

Tough's hand, still pink and scabbed, with not a spot of black grease, sat easily on Kelly's shoulder. She resisted the urge to snuggle back into his chest or grab his hand and lace his fingers with her own.

If Torque and Cassidy thought it strange that the entire bridal party continued to stand on the steps as they moved toward the car and the guests came spilling out of the church, they didn't let on.

It was easy to tell when Torque noticed the cereal. He paused, mid-stride. Then turned and looked straight at Turbo, who was completely prepared for that reaction, having experienced it before, apparently. He raised his hands in innocence and pointed directly at Kelly. Kelly, who had never done anything like that before in her life, was most definitely not prepared and stood with wide eyes, a gaping mouth, and the guiltiest look possible on her face.

Cassidy and Torque shared a look of shock. Tough shifted behind her, and she realized he was silently telling Torque, *Come on, do you really think Turbo had nothing to do with this?*

Torque just grinned and rolled his eyes. He opened Cassidy's car door, and piles of cereal fell to the ground. They scooped out enough for her to get in, and the guests cheered when he finally closed the door around her.

Torque did the same to his side and started the car. He pulled slowly out to the road.

Even though Kelly was expecting the horn to honk, she wasn't expecting it to be such an earsplitting, deafening sound. When the brake lights came on, the horn gave such a thunderous blast it would have blown her socks off, if she'd been wearing any. She jumped back, and Tough's arms came around her. A few seconds later, she felt Tough's phone buzz.

He kept one arm around her while he pulled his phone out and held it so she could read Torque's text.

The horn was not Turbo.

Tough texted back with one hand.

It was Kelly.

Kelly gasped. "It was not!"

Not believing it.

She handed me the tools. 😊

Kelly laughed. "Now that's true. I really didn't know what you guys were getting me into."

Torque must have decided to go with it, because no more texts came and he pulled out, tapping the brakes twice more just for fun.

Tough's phone buzzed one more time.

That was good. Cassidy is laughing.

Kelly turned her head and met Tough's laughing eyes, sharing the warmth of laughter and fun. Something passed between them, something in his swirling brown eyes. Her smile froze, and her lungs felt tight.

Would she laugh like this with Preston?

Her face must have shown her confusion, because Tough's look went from happy to concerned. His brows furrowed. "What?"

"Is this your life?"

"What?" His brows pinched. "No. First wedding."

Kelly shook her head. Someone bumped her from behind with a mumbled "excuse me." "No, I mean..." She meant the fun and the laughter, goofing off and good-natured ribbing. "Never mind. I guess we'd better get to the reception."

"You can ride with me if you want," Tough said.

Her brows lifted. "Um, no. I'd need to come back and get my car. I'd better take myself."

"Okay." He shrugged. "See ya there."

But he didn't move until she'd gotten in her car and driven away.

# Chapter Twelve

The reception was casual, held in a fire hall. It was nicely decorated but not fancy, making it comfortable for the kids. The food was wholesome and tasty without being fussy or pretentious. Kelly sat with Dusty and Harris at the head table and laughed so hard she cried more than once. Cassidy and Torque looked so happy together. Some of Torque's hardness had melted away, whether from love or from the laughter of friends and family, she wasn't sure.

Harris leaned over and said softly in Kelly's ear, "There. You can't look at them and tell me you don't believe in love."

"Oh, I believe in it now. Just I've seen so many couples who were so happy as they got married, but then it vanished in a bitter divorce and custody battle. And the children lose. Every time. I've seen it so much… too much," Kelly finished softly, her heart clenching for the children who would never stop wishing and hoping that their parents would get back together. Or, worse, for the ones who wondered what was wrong with them and why their parents left and didn't want them.

"I guess with your work, you would. I see it some too, at the library. But I can't keep from believing that they will be one of the ones who make it work to the end. You know?" Harris's serious eyes blinked.

"I want to believe that and for myself too, but the statistics aren't really for that. And I would hate to see my own children suffer."

"So what makes you think that you and Preston won't split?" Harris asked matter-of-factly.

It wasn't hard. "Because we're going into it with our eyes open. We're not basing things on wishy-washy feelings of physical, passionate love, which obviously can die or fade away or whatever."

"But can't that go wrong too? Can't one of you decide that your agreement isn't working anymore? You don't have to fall out of love to split. Companies split all the time. Churches split. People leave their gyms, their places of employment, they move because they can't get along with the neighbors that they used to be best friends with... It doesn't have to be love."

Kelly played with the bit of tulle on the table. She hadn't thought of it that way. "I wrote to Dr. T last night."

Harris's eyes brightened. "Really? Wow. Please, please, please, let me know what he says. Did you sign your real name?"

Kelly put her hand on her forehead. "Uh, I never even thought about signing a different name. Oh, my gosh. I should have, shouldn't I? I'm so dumb sometimes!"

"Maybe he won't print it."

"Not with my luck."

The DJ announced it was time for the wedding party to have the first dance. Colton came over and offered his hand to Harris. "Think about it," she said as she stood.

Harris walked away, and Dusty was getting up beside a grinning Turbo, but when Kelly looked around, Tough still sat in his chair. He had both hands on the table and was watching them like the Hail Mary pass of a tied Super Bowl.

So, Tough didn't dance. Great. Some part of her she didn't want to examine too closely was more disappointed that she would miss dancing with him than upset that she'd be sitting here awkwardly through the whole song.

"Kelly?" Tough's voice broke into her thoughts. She looked up, her heart thumping. She lifted a hand to her chest in surprise. She hadn't expected him to walk over.

He seemed just as confident as he always did. Easy set to the shoulders that were now minus the suit coat. His sleeves were rolled up partway, and his brown arms contrasted with the white shirt in a way that set her heart racing. Still, it was there in the eyes that stared straight into hers. Uncertainty. That she'd refuse him, maybe? Hesitation. Maybe fear. She almost snorted. He'd obviously faced his fear. The very fact that he was standing here, in front of all these people, waiting for her to accept his offer, and the fact that he was willing to dance in front of them if she accepted showed that.

She smiled and stood, and some of the tightness around his face and mouth eased.

"You look amazing." The words were out before she could stop them as she placed her hand in his.

"That's what I was thinking about you." His words sent a thrill down her spine, and her hand tingled as it rested in his. "I guess I'd better warn you that I've never danced before."

"What? Never?" She stepped into his arms, as natural as breathing.

He began to sway, slowly. "No."

"What about high school? What about those dances?"

"I asked a girl once, and she told me no." His eyes crinkled slightly at the corners, although his expression stayed serious. "I didn't really want to go anyway. Not without her."

There was that burning again. Jealousy. She would never have called herself a jealous person. "Who did you ask?"

"Eh, it was back in seventh grade. I guess I thought I was grown up and she was too."

"So you really liked her?" He must have to have asked her to a dance.

"Yeah." Just one word, breathed out softly, but it was so heavy, so full of things he wasn't saying.

"You still like her?"

His pristine white shirt rose and fell as he took a deep breath and let it out slow. "Yeah."

Acid, hot and burning, exploded in her stomach. There was no other word for it; she was jealous, insanely jealous of this girl, now woman, whom Tough liked. Who had told him no. Who had been the only other woman he'd asked to dance with. Of course, he was only dancing with Kelly because they had to.

"Who was she?" The question came out more like a demand.

He looked down, and the eddy of his brown eyes was deeper than she could have guessed. "You."

She stopped dancing. He stopped with her. She shook her head in denial, even as she sorted through her childhood memories. Tough had never asked her to a dance. They didn't even go to the same school. "No. It wasn't me. You never asked me."

His hands put pressure on her shoulders, and she began moving again, woodenly. His hands slipped around her waist.

"I did."

"When? How? Where were we?"

"You were at Preston's house."

That made sense. That's pretty much where she lived.

"You were with a crowd of friends. I walked, man, it was several hours from where I lived then to Preston's house. I wasn't going to ask you in front of all of them, but they saw me."

Realization came over Kelly the way a flood turns a river brown. "I never spoke with you. They just shouted over to where I was sitting on the pavilion that some boy was walking down the street and wanted to take me to a dance." She'd caught a glimpse of him—torn jeans, ratty t-shirt, scuffed shoes, tall, and skinny, she remembered vaguely now. "I hadn't known it was you."

His finger rubbed over her back. "You wouldn't have known me anyway."

She shivered from the light touch that spread fire through her blood. "I would've remembered you. How could I forget the boy who'd saved me?"

"It wouldn't have mattered. I can see it now, but at the time, I thought...I guess I thought...I don't know what I thought." He shook his head, and for the first time, he broke eye contact, looking over her shoulder the way he had when they first met.

Her heart constricted. Could hearts cry? That's what it felt like, like her heart was crying, but her eyes remained dry. Obviously, he believed she would have turned him down, even if he'd been able to ask her directly, even if she'd known who he was. Would she?

She had been deeply entrenched in the popular, wealthy lifestyle, but she'd never, not once, lost sight of where she'd come from or what she wanted to do when she was able. She'd also never forgotten the dirty, scrappy, quiet little boy who'd taken her where he knew someone wanted her.

"I would have said yes, if I'd known it was you." She said it with confidence because she knew it was true. She'd never cared at all what everyone else thought. She'd been focused on helping other people. Always.

Tough looked back down at her. "I believe you. But I also think you made the right choice."

There seemed to be more to his words, a meaning that she wasn't sure she really understood, because he didn't know what she was struggling with, didn't know that she had to make another, similar choice. But his tone almost implied that he did and that he thought she should not choose him again. How could that be?

The song ended. For a space, his arms seemed to tighten, like he didn't want to let her go, but then they dropped. White teeth contrasted with the dark tan and eyes, and it raised his level of handsomeness to a whole new point.

"The dance was worth the wait. Thanks." He took her elbow and guided her to her chair, where he'd found her, leaving her there.

The rest of the reception went by in a haze. She caught a glimpse of Tough dancing with one twin in each arm and another of him grinning, yes, *grinning*, at Torque and slapping him on the back.

And then it was over, and she went home, alone.

# Chapter Thirteen

Tough couldn't believe he'd admitted so much to Kelly. He'd practically told her he'd been in love with her all his life. Which, now that he thought about it, was probably true. He'd also practically told her that he knew she had a choice to make and, although it would hurt him, he wanted her to make the right choice. The choice she'd made before.

His chest hurt from the war between his head and heart. Kelly needed to choose, should choose someone else. But every smile she sent his way, every touch, every moment he spent with her made him long for and hope for her to choose him. The war inside his body wouldn't stop.

Still, there was a glow in his heart that he just couldn't shake, not that he wanted to. He felt light and happy like he hadn't felt in years. Who was he kidding? Hadn't felt in forever.

"You're humming today?" Mr. Sigel barked from the checker table.

He was. He was humming. The song, whatever it was, that he'd danced to with Kelly. He was humming that song. "Nope. Must be your hearing aid acting up again," he hollered across the garage.

"Hurumph," Mr. Sigel said before turning back to his checkers and a thoughtful Al, who nodded.

"He was humming." Al picked up his red king and jumped Mr. Sigel's only king.

Tough wiped off a wrench. Kelly would be over on the other side tonight, and he'd help her renovate, he'd enjoy every second, and soon she'd be moving in with her passel of kids.

He jerked at the thought, banging his head on the tire of the car on the lift. She'd choose Preston, and he'd have to live and work with Kelly every day. No. No way. He couldn't do that. He'd definitely have to think of something. Moving the garage or...something.

That's what had to happen. Her life going in one direction, his in another. Depressing.

He wasn't going to let it get him down today, though. He was definitely basking in the afterglow.

Right at five, Kelly walked into the shop. He'd never seen her in jeans and a tee before. It threw him off a little because she looked good. More than good. Never in his life had he been tempted to put his tools down and go hug someone, but he fought that urge today.

"Be done here in a minute," he called. He didn't like to leave a messy shop.

"I hope you don't mind, but Dusty is coming later and bringing pizza."

"This boy don't turn food down," Mr. Sigel said.

"Oh, are you helping?" Kelly asked with a smile.

"I'm supervising. Off the clock. I'm union."

"You *were* union," Al said. "Not something to be proud of, necessarily." He pointed a finger at his own chest. "I am actually helping."

Tough walked to the sink and squirted degreaser on his hands, rubbing it up his arms to his t-shirt sleeves. "Al was a contractor before he sold his business and retired. He helped me make the walls in here, hang the ceiling, do the wiring and plumbing." He waved his arm around, indicating the whole garage.

"The crooked doorjambs are not my fault. The building isn't square."

"Oh." Kelly nodded, and Tough snorted.

"It's the reason you fell in my office that day."

Kelly's head jerked up. Something flashed across her face. Maybe she was remembering that he'd caught her, that they'd been tangled up, that he'd seen all of her long, shapely leg.

He looked away first and finished rinsing off his hands and arms. The degreaser took off the better part of the day's grime, but if he wanted to be truly clean—no grease at all—he had to cut skin. He'd done it for the wedding, and he often did it for church, but not for too much else. Working with Kelly? If he had time, he figured he would. There wasn't too much he wouldn't do for her. Unfortunately, there was a lot he *couldn't* do. If only his stupid heart could remember that.

The old men shuffled over with Kelly. Tough followed after shutting everything down and flipping the "CLOSED" sign over.

He'd done handyman work before, he'd even done jobs in high school with Al, but he was glad of Al's presence, because he took one look at the room and didn't have the foggiest idea of where to begin. He supposed that was the way some people felt when they lifted the hood of their car—nothing made sense to them. So, as Al gave orders, he gladly obeyed, doing mostly the grunt work of carrying large, heavy pieces of garbage out to the dumpster they'd had delivered when Kelly signed the papers. He also ran some air hoses and extension cords through from the shop to run the saws and other power tools.

It was dark and turning chilly by the time Dusty arrived with the pizza. They sat on buckets of spackling and boxes of screws.

"You can keep carrying everything out," Al said between bites. "Once we get it all gutted, then we get started with the fun stuff."

"Okay. I can keep working on it in the evenings. I might even be able to get some time in before work," Kelly said. "I want to get it finished as fast as we can. Every day it's not open is a day that the kids couldn't be here and be safe."

"If you can get the boy here out of bed, maybe he'd come over and help you," Mr. Sigel said gruffly but with an affectionate twinkle in his eye.

"I might be able to drag my bones out by noontime. What time does work start, two?" Tough ribbed Mr. Sigel.

"Honestly, boy, don't know what I'm gonna do with you. Never amount to anything if you can't get up in the morning." Mr. Sigel waved his half-empty coffee cup around.

They joked a little until Dusty spoke up, "Oh, Kelly. Did you hear? Someone on the news said that they've figured out who Dr. T is! They're going to 'unmask' him at some big show on TV. Maybe they're trying to drum up viewers." She laughed a little and bounced in her seat.

"Oh, wow. Now we'll finally know if it's a he or a she."

"It's a she," Harris said with confidence.

"Who's Dr. T?" Mr. Sigel asked.

Dusty launched into an explanation, helped by Kelly, while Tough sat, stunned. They knew who he was? Did it have something to do with him going to daily posts? Had they traced him through his credit card processor? Surely they would have contacted him and told him. He couldn't say for sure.

Anxiety tightened his chest, pulled at his muscles. Not only that he would lose income he was counting on to keep helping his elderly patrons because people wouldn't think a mechanic with no background in psychology and no actual experience in relationships could run an advice column, but also because...people would want him to talk. There would be video cameras, news people, interview requests.

He realized his jaw was locked, and he deliberately loosened it. He looked up to see Kelly considering him. "You don't like advice columns?"

Oh, wow. He was skating on thin ice here. "Car columns."

She lowered her head. "Relationship columns."

He spread his arms, indicating his garage and the old men. "Don't need 'em."

"This is all you want out of life?" she asked softly. "Didn't seeing Torque get married make you want...more?"

It had. Of course it had. He'd always wanted more, wanted Kelly. But she wasn't for him, and he'd accepted that long ago. Plus, he'd loved his mother, and she'd died. That was the way his life went. "Didn't change anything." Which was the truth.

"Well, it's about time to get my old bones in bed," Al said as he stood up.

They cleaned up the garbage from the pizza. Tough caught Kelly alone as he walked it out to the dumpster. "What time you coming in the morning? I'll help."

She stopped, her blond hair bouncing as she shook her head. "I couldn't ask you to do that. I already appreciate your help so much. It doesn't take any special skill to get this place cleaned up."

"What time?"

She laughed. He loved that sound.

"I can make it by five. That gives me a good three and a half hours before I have to be at work."

"I'll be here." He snorted. "I'll be up."

"Right. Since you'll already be here."

He stopped, resisting the urge to touch her, to pull her close. "I'll wait and make sure you get in your car okay."

She looked like she was going to argue, but she just said, "Thanks."

He watched her walk away, the jeans doing something odd to his insides, and wished it were possible for her to be his.

"I didn't pack a lunch, but my stomach is telling me it's time to take a break." Kelly stood on a ladder, painting the walls. It was Saturday, and she was impressed with the amount of work they'd gotten done. She really didn't know where Tough got all his energy, either. He'd work from five in the morning until after she left at nine most nights.

"It's 12," he said, shoving the drill back into the tool belt he wore around his slim waist.

"Is there anywhere around where we can eat? My treat."

"I'll take you to Pop's. It's just up the street."

Tough took her painting things to his shop to rinse them out, while she closed the can and tidied things up. She hurried over to wash her hands.

"How far is Pop's?" she asked.

"Just up the street a block. The owners are Greek, and they've got some good stuff."

They put jackets on against the late October chill and stepped out.

Her hand brushed Tough's, and he jerked, turning to look at her. "Sorry," he said.

She shrugged.

He studied her for a moment. She smiled.

They waited at the corner for a slow car, and Tough touched her hand again. This time, he didn't apologize.

Their fingers touched, twisted, and by the time they started across the street, her hand nestled in his. She didn't pull away, and neither did he as they walked along.

She liked the feeling, his hand holding hers, but didn't want to examine it too closely. Preston was always in the back of her mind. She had to talk to him, had to figure out where they were going. Phone service and times had been spotty. She might have been able to break it off with him while he was gone but not with a text. Guilt twisted in her chest, but she pushed it aside. When Preston got home, she would deal with their agreement.

Instead she relished the warm safety that she always felt when with Tough, even more now that he held her hand.

He stopped at a small store, right on the sidewalk. *Pop's* was painted in blue letters over the door. Store advertisements and specials lined the door and the lower part of the large windows along the sidewalk. Tough opened the door with his free hand and held it while she walked in. He didn't let go of her, and she didn't try to get her hand back. It was too nice holding it. She didn't want to think any farther than that.

A dark-haired man with a big, round belly greeted them. "Tough. You are here once again. And you have a pretty girl with you. That is new, no?"

Kelly could swear the tips of Tough's ears turned pink, but his face remained calm. "I got me a pretty one today, Bemus. I wanna feed her. You'll help me out?" Tough asked.

"Oh, sure. That is what we do."

The menu was above the counter, and Kelly studied it. "We order here," Tough said to her, "and pay. And then we choose our seat, and they bring it to us."

"Okay."

Tough ordered and bantered some with Bemus, which gave Kelly time to peruse the menu so she was ready to order when he asked. After paying, Tough grabbed plasticware, napkins, and her hand and led her around the corner to a small alcove tucked in the back.

Kelly slid into her chair at the small table. Grape leaves hung on the walls, and although the table was out of sight for most of the restaurant, it didn't feel claustrophobic or dark. "I love this table," she said as Tough sat down across from her. "If I'd been here myself," who was she kidding, she would have never come in here on her own, "I wouldn't have taken the time to find this table."

Tough lifted a shoulder. "Suits me."

Kelly snorted. "That's an understatement."

Tough seemed to consider whether she was serious or not, then he said, "Food's good. It's what counts."

She tilted her head, looking at the various plants that gave the restaurant an outdoorsy feel. "In a restaurant, I supposed you're right."

Tough followed her gaze before looking back at her. "I'm not going to be able to help you this Saturday."

"Oh, hot date?" The words slipped out of her mouth, and she wished she could grab them and shove them back in.

But his lips twitched, and he said, "Maybe." He looked down and fiddled with his napkin, before he met her eyes again. "I was going to ask you if you wanted to come."

"Oh." Her stomach dropped.

"It's a charity truck pull. I usually take the tow truck and volunteer mechanical services." He twisted the napkin tighter around the silverware before he set them down and carefully folded his hands on the table.

Kelly drew her brows together. "A charity truck pull? Never heard of it."

"It's just organized by local folks. Guys take their trucks and pull, people pay to see it, and most of the expenses are donated by the organizers and the drivers."

"Who benefits?"

Tough shifted, picking up his silverware again and unwrapping it. "Typically, some driver or puller or someone we know who's going through a hard time. This year, it's a fellow with inoperable cancer who has a wife and five kids. They're doing chemo but don't have a lot of hope for him."

Wow, for a really good cause. "Oh. What can I do?"

He folded his napkin and carefully pushed the crease down.

Bemus bustled over and set their food on the table. "Very romantic back here, yes?"

"It is romantic," Kelly agreed. Private and romantic. It was definitely the best table in the restaurant. Kelly smiled at him. "The food looks delicious."

"Thank you. Eat. Enjoy." He patted Tough on the shoulder and winked at him before walking away.

Kelly surveyed the delicious-looking food in front of her before she teased Tough, "Does he do that every time you bring a girl in?"

"Don't know." Tough picked up his gyro. "It's good food."

"You were telling me what I could do at the truck pull."

He studied his gyro like he needed to find the key to eat it properly. Finally, he sighed. "I just thought you might enjoy it. It's for a good cause, but it's also fun. I thought it might be nice to bring a friend and have a fun day with her." He lifted his eyes at that last comment, and Kelly was caught again in the dark color that had no bottom.

"I'd love to." Her voice sounded husky, and the sultry note had crept back in.

Tough's eyes flickered, and he nodded before taking a bite.

"What time?"

He finished chewing and swallowed before he answered. "It starts at noon, so we could get some work done in the morning before we leave. Takes an hour to get there. I'd say 10:30. They'll quit at dark."

"It gets cold after dark."

He nodded. "That and the fairground doesn't charge to use their facility if they don't turn the lights on. Someone usually gives a donation so they open the restrooms."

"Will there be food?" Kelly asked. She could pack something.

"Yeah, someone usually sets up a stand and donates the profits to the family."

They thought of everything. "Wow. Sounds like a big deal."

"Everyone does something. They donate what they have."

Kelly thought of the big charities she worked for and the rich donors they had. Sometimes it seemed like people just threw money and assumed that the work got done. "So everyone pitches in?"

"Yeah."

"So I should do something." She didn't want to be standing around with nothing to do.

"You're gonna be with me."

"That's enough?"

His hands stilled with the gyro midair, and his eyes met hers. Her chest tightened, and she realized how their last statements could be used for their relationship in general. Tough didn't feel like he was enough for her. She'd never indicated any different. Honestly, she wasn't sure. Was he? Was being with Tough worth giving up everything she'd ever wanted for the thin hope of something better?

Patrons talked, glasses and dishes clanked, but in the alcove, those sounds faded into the background, and Kelly was hyperaware of Tough's every breath, shallow and a little fast. The pulse in his neck beat in and out. His left eye ticked.

Kelly's throat felt tight, and her ribcage seemed to compress. Tough seemed to be waiting for her to say something, although she'd asked the last question, and she didn't know what the right answer was.

She blinked and looked down. The moment passed. She couldn't give him something she wasn't sure of herself.

<h1 style="text-align:center">Chapter Fourteen</h1>

Saturday dawned clear and bright. Tough knew it, because he was outside to see the sunrise. He'd actually been up before the sunrise and finished writing a week's worth of answers for his now daily column. The increase in income had been greater than he'd expected, and he knew exactly what he was going to do with it.

As for the "unmasking," he'd been in touch with his agent. They hadn't heard anything concrete, but he'd had an idea that might spin things in their direction. Sure, it made him sick to his stomach to think about it, so he decided he wouldn't. He knew he could handle it if he didn't allow himself to dwell on it.

What he didn't know was whether he did the right thing in answering Kelly's question. He'd struggled, putting together several answers, deleting each one. A professional, he knew, would have excused himself because of being too close to the situation. He'd considered doing that too. Maybe it's what he should have done. It wouldn't be the first time in his life that he'd done something he shouldn't have.

He took a sip of his coffee, pondering.

Regardless, on Monday, Kelly's question and his answer would be posted on his advice column. It was sure to receive attention, more than usual, since it was the first time he'd answered a woman. The column had started out as a mechanic's advice column, but he'd been good, better even, at answering relationship issues. There hadn't been many women. He didn't feel qualified to tell them what to do, anyway. It was far easier to straight-talk a man. Still, he couldn't ignore Kelly. Just couldn't. Even if it was wrong.

He took a moment to admire the bright orange, yellow, and pink sky beyond the dusty old buildings that lined his street and take a deep breath of the crisp, early morning air. Kelly had agreed to spend the day with him. As a friend, of course. He'd been thinking for a while now that he was probably in love with her. Had probably been in love with her for years, if not since kindergarten. But he couldn't let on. Couldn't spoil the day by making her uncomfortable and pushing her away from him. Monday would come soon enough.

The sky had become more blue than orange, and Tough was about to walk back in when a familiar car pulled down the street. Mr. Millard. Odd to have him out in the middle of the month. He usually showed up conveniently close to the end, and Tough never had to mail his check, but this was definitely an odd turn of events.

The car slowed to a stop, edging toward the curb in front of Tough. Tough sipped his coffee then moseyed over when Mr. Millard put his window down.

"Tough, figured I'd catch you up this early."

Tough nodded, waiting.

Mr. Millard tapped the steering wheel. "I just wanted to let you know I'm selling the building. Didn't know if you'd be interested."

Heck, yeah. He was interested.

"How much?"

Mr. Millard named the figure, and Tough's shoulders slumped. Couldn't afford it. Not in this life.

"Love to, but can't."

"I figured. Hated to see her evicted, but felt it was fair to ask first."

Wait. "You have a buyer?"

"Yeah. Wasn't really thinking of selling. But this guy with this string of nightclubs approached me. Guess he saw the "For Rent" sign. He didn't want to rent, though. Can't blame him. Anyway, about a week ago, he made me an offer to buy. Good offer." Yeah. With that kind of money, Mr. Millard could retire to Florida and live the rest of his life carefree. "But the wife said it was only fair to give you the chance to match it. You've been the perfect renter for the last ten years. We've got other properties, but no one pays the rent like you."

Tough nodded, his mind scrambling. Where would he go? What about Kelly and her half-finished renovations? Was she out that money?

"He won't be able to kick her out right away. State laws and such. Seemed like a decent guy too. She's got a few months to find a new place."

But where? The economy had caused all the old, empty warehouses to fill up. He couldn't think of a single place for rent. His heart bled for Kelly and her hopes of having a children's center here, where so many of her kids lived. It wouldn't be easy for either of them to find a place. He didn't even want to think about the fact that the idea of not seeing Kelly every day was almost worse than losing his garage.

"I'll keep my eyes open for you if you want me to."

"'Preciate it." Tough took a deeper drink of his coffee and saw that the orange had completely bled out of the sky. The day had officially begun. And he was officially on notice that he needed to find a new place.

Wait. "You're saying 'she.' Does he only need one side?"

Mr. Millard's bald head nodded. The sun reflected orange off it. "Yep, that's what he said. My terms were that he had to let you stay and evict the new renter, Kelly. He agreed. Don't worry. He's going to offer you a contract. You're set for the next ten years."

"Give it to Kelly."

Mr. Millard jerked his head around. "What?"

"Have him put the nightclub on my side. It's on the busier street anyway." Kelly might not be happy about having her children next to a nightclub, but it was probably better than having no place.

Moving one hand from the steering wheel to his forehead, Mr. Millard said, "I'm not understanding. You're giving up your side of the warehouse, and you want the new girl to stay?"

"Yeah."

He waved his hand in the air. "You're never going to find another place. Not around here. Your clientele won't follow you to a new town."

True. Tough though of Mr. Sigel and Al. Of all the elderly folk that came in for free oil changes, tires, and repairs. They were so often faced with the choice of paying their property taxes or having a car, and he liked to think he'd helped many of them do both. But now… He told himself there would be elderly people wherever he found a place. He just hated leaving the ones here that had become his family over the years. But the other choice was even harder. He could never allow Kelly to be evicted while he stayed.

"No. Kelly stays. Find out from the buyer when he's closing and tell him I'll be out the day he wants to move in. Just let me know."

Mr. Millard stared at him. "Why are you doing this?"

"She's building a place for children to come and be off the streets. For them to be safe, cared for, and out of trouble." Tough couldn't allow that to slip from her.

"But you've got people who have been depending on you for years." Mr. Millard stared at his hands on the wheel.

"I didn't ask for that. It just happened." Which was the truth. The men just showed up, and they somehow stayed. Sure, he paid them some when they picked up parts and even when they didn't, he tried to slip them something to supplement their social security, but still, he'd never asked for them to come or help.

"Funny that it hasn't 'just happened' to any other mechanic or body shop I know."

"Just make sure that Kelly gets that ten-year contract, okay?"

Mr. Millard nodded. Tough finished his coffee, bitter and cold, before he walked in to get started.

KELLY HADN'T EXPECTED THERE to be so many people at the truck pull. She had been thinking it was just a group of guys getting together to have fun. But the fairground track was packed. Long lines snaked out of the makeshift concession stands, which, instead of hot sausages and cactus fries, had meatballs, BBQ chicken, and chili. Homemade food with the big, handwritten signs declaring it wasn't expensive, either.

The grandstands were packed, and men on tractors and a roller ran over the track.

A little shot of anxiety popped in her chest. Would anyone recognize her? Would Preston be hurt that she didn't tell him what she was doing? At least not before she was able to talk to him?

She pushed it aside. These were hardly the type of people who ran in Preston's circles.

Her circles.

She refused to worry about it, even though the number of people here far exceeded her expectations. She was going to enjoy herself today. With Tough.

As they bumped across an old hayfield in Tough's tow truck, people waved and called out, then took a second look. It made her smile, the faces of people when they saw Tough had a woman with him.

"I love how people stare at you once they see me."

Tough's eyes moved back and forth as he maneuvered the truck around several parked rigs and waited for a couple of kids to scatter out of the way. "They're just wondering how I managed to get enough words out of my mouth to get you in my truck. They probably think I threw you over my shoulder and tossed you in. Don't be surprised if someone asks if you need to be rescued."

She chuckled. "No one's going to ask that. I think most of them are happy for you. More probably will be once they get over their shock."

Tough snorted. He pulled the truck to a stop at the gate where a lady with a money apron took his cash and gave him a ticket.

Wood smoke, tangy BBQ chicken, and diesel exhaust mixed together and blew in the open window. A fellow in a ball cap wearing worn overalls and work boots, holding a drink in one hand and a meatball sandwich in the other, waved them forward with the meatball sandwich and stopped them next to the track.

Before Tough could get out, the man hurried over, chewing, and stuck his head in the window. "You mind getting...oh, 'scuse me." He used his drink to tip his cap at Kelly.

"Sure," she said with a smile.

"Uh, anyway, Tough, you mind climbing on the tractor with the chisel plow yonder? Jeff was on it, but he had to go turn the chicken.

Looks to me like he's dealing with a grease fire too. We need to get this track done." He swallowed and took another bite which made almost half the sandwich disappear.

"Yeah."

"Does the lady drive? We need someone in the water truck."

"She'll ride with me. Drive the water truck yourself." Tough softened his words with an eye crinkle.

The man sighed. "I know. Just won't have time to eat later, and everything was gone last year 'til we were done."

Tough lifted a brow. "Looks like you could skip a few meals."

"Shut up. Plus, if I'm not here to park people, it'll look like a traffic jam 'til I get back."

Tough rolled his eyes. "We'll run the plow."

"Thanks." The guy popped the rest of the sub in his mouth and disappeared from the window.

Kelly grabbed Tough's arm. "Won't he need to give you the keys?"

"Keys'll be in the ignition. Unless I need to hotwire it. Then there'll be a screwdriver somewhere, probably under the seat, in that case."

"Okay," Kelly said doubtfully.

"Coming?" Tough asked as he hopped out.

Grabbing her jacket, Kelly stepped out and walked around the front of the truck. Tough, with his ball cap pulled low, his biceps straining his tee, and his worn jeans and work boots, looked good enough to draw a crowd himself. He stopped in front of her. She couldn't see his eyes through the mirror shades, but his brows bunched.

"Are you okay? You mind running the tractor with me?"

"I'll tell you if I mind." She tilted her head. "I'm planning on spending the day with you and having a good time. If that means I'm going to do something with a tractor, I'm going to enjoy the new experience."

She was rewarded with a small flash of white teeth, which, against his dark skin, made her heart flutter.

He grabbed her hand, and she followed him with a warm happiness in her heart.

"You'll sit here." He patted the fender over the tire that was as tall as her.

Keeping a hold of her hand, he put his other hand on her waist and helped her balance as she climbed up the metal steps. Heat flowed from his hand to her waist. She turned on the small platform and squeezed between the seat and the fender, sitting gingerly on the cool metal. He climbed up behind her, squeezed between her legs and the steering wheel, and sat in the springy metal seat.

"You can hold onto the fender here." He showed her how she could grip. "The tire's under it, but you'll be fine, there's several inches' clearance, and that won't move. I promise." Another little flash of white accompanied this statement, and although his words didn't really reassure her, his almost-smile did. "You can hold the back of my seat with your other hand, or you can hold onto me anywhere you need to. Don't grab the steering wheel."

"I think I knew that," Kelly said.

"You good?"

"If I feel like I'm going to fall off, will you stop?"

There was no hint of humor on his face when he said, "You're not going to fall off the tractor."

"Okay?"

He took her hand that was gripped on the back of his seat and wrapped her fingers around his arm. Hard, warm, solid muscle. "Don't let go."

She swallowed. Nodded.

He turned back and focused his attention on the knobs and controls. His hands moved with confidence as he adjusted the shifter and another knob, depressed a pedal with each foot, then turned the key. When nothing happened, he felt around under the seat and pulled out a screwdriver.

Kelly jumped as sparks flew. A rumble, then black smoke shot out the exhaust on the hood, then the motor roared to life. Tough put the screwdriver back. "Sorry. Should have warned you about the sparks."

"Yes." Her heart settled down, back inside her chest.

"I'm not going to let anything happen to you."

"I trust you." For some reason she couldn't explain.

He shifted the machine into gear and slowly let the clutch out. The tractor bounced into motion.

After a few passes up and down the track, where she never once felt like she was going to fall off and get plowed into the track, Kelly started to relax and enjoy the beautiful, sunny day. She turned her face to the deep, rich blue sky and the sparkling sun which turned the Appalachian Mountains in the distance an opulent burnt gold. The slight breeze lifted her hair and brought the fresh smell of deep woods to the valley.

"I feel like a hillbilly, riding like this," she said to Tough. Her hand hadn't moved from his arm. As he maneuvered the controls, the muscles under her fingers flexed and bunched, and she figured that more than one girl would love to trade places with her. She felt lucky to be alive on such a gorgeous day and blessed to be spending the day with a man like Tough. It was all icing that they were doing it for a good cause.

"Guess ya kinda are. For today anyway," he replied. His head nodded over toward the firepit where the second batch of barbeque chicken was cooking. "See the skinny guy in the green hat and red shirt?"

"The one holding a little girl in ponytails?" she asked.

Tough glanced over. "Yeah. He's got a couple more little kids standing around him."

"Yes?" she asked.

"That's Ryan."

"The man with cancer?" He did look thin. And tired.

"Yeah. I'll introduce you later. His wife's the one behind the baby stroller."

"Oh my. Is that their baby?"

"Yeah. It's about six months old, I think. He was diagnosed 'bout a month or so before it was born."

Kelly's heart hurt. "Wow. That's rough."

"It's even rougher that he hasn't been able to work because of the treatments."

"Oh." Kelly squinted. The wife had her hair in a ponytail, but it was a shade of orange that was kind of unforgettable. "You just fixed their car last week."

The woman's hair had been down the day Kelly had seen her. She had the baby with her too.

"Yeah."

Tough didn't say any more, and Kelly didn't pry, but if she remembered correctly, the woman had been crying. Tough had put something white in her hand, which seemed like an odd way to hand someone a bill, but Kelly had been distracted...

Then it clicked. "You didn't charge her."

Tough worked the pedals and shifted into reverse. He answered without stopping. "Of course not."

"You gave her money."

"Might've." His shoulder lifted slightly, but he kept his eyes on the track and the tractor moving.

She thought about the bags of groceries that Mr. Sigel and Al had brought in and set down in the corner. They'd disappeared.

"You gave her groceries."

"Did I?"

"You did! You had Mr. Sigel and Al go buy her groceries."

He let go of the steering wheel to poke her shoulder. "Nosy neighbor."

She laughed. She had to admit she loved the feel of his muscles as he drove the tractor, and she could admire him for a long time in his jeans and work boots, but his character ran through him like a vein of gold in the Yukon. Suddenly she didn't care that she might look like a redneck hillbilly. She leaned her head back and laughed, loud and long, a belly laugh that bubbled up from the happiest, most joyful depths of her soul. Was it possible to be happier?

"You crazy, lady?"

With the wind blowing her hair and joy spilling out of every pore of her body, she laughed again. "I am. Crazy."

<h1 style="text-align:center">Chapter Fifteen</h1>

They stayed until after dark. They didn't use the fair lights, but someone had brought industrial work lights, plus several trucks, including Tough's tow truck, had work lights attached.

Tough hadn't realized how much better things could be with a smart and funny woman beside him. He'd thought he enjoyed his life before, but after spending the day with Kelly, it was hard to imagine anything ever being fun without her again.

They grabbed the last of the garbage bags and threw them in the back of Ralph's truck. Most everyone else had already pulled out, leaving just Ralph and the couple who had run the food booth.

"Can't believe we made that much money to give to Jeff. His wife couldn't stop crying," Ralph said as he shut the tailgate.

Tough figured she probably hadn't stopped crying much since her husband's diagnosis, but he didn't say that. Just nodded.

Ralph clamped him on the shoulder. "Thanks for your help. You should treat your girl to some ice cream or something."

Tough looked over at Kelly who had just finished helping to carry the last of the food tables to the truck. She'd helped to pack up the leftover food and send it home with Jeff's family while he'd gotten caught up in emptying garbage cans and cleaning the bathrooms. Just before dark, it had gotten chilly, and he'd gone to his truck and given her his jacket. It stirred every possessive instinct in his caveman heart to see her wearing his coat.

"She's a good girl," Ralph finally said, when Tough didn't answer.

He agreed. But he had to say, "She's not mine."

"Oh." The bushy brows almost touched the ball cap Ralph wore. "You looked so comfortable together, I just thought…"

"No. Just a friend." No matter how much he wanted it to be more.

Ralph kept watching Kelly, who laughed with the family and gave the woman a hand lifting a bulky roaster into the back of their truck. "Wish I had a 'friend' like that. The wife got her hair done today."

"Take her some flowers home," Tough said. Kelly leaned over the edge of the truck to arrange something on the bed. His jacket rode up, and his eyes lingered on her soft curves and long legs before he fished his phone out of his pocket and checked the time.

Ralph rolled his eyes. "Humph. They wouldn't be the right kind or the right color, or she'd be allergic."

"Try candy." Tough's eyes tracked back to Kelly.

"She's on a diet."

"Tell her that her hair looks nice and wash the dishes."

"I'm not allowed to touch the dishes because I don't do them right."

"Rub her feet."

"She hates her feet. She thinks they're ugly."

Tough finally looked at Ralph. There had to be something. "What makes her happy?"

"Having me gone." Ralph shrugged. "It's why I'm here. Can't do anything else right."

Wow. Sometimes there was just nothing to do to help. But he'd keep trying. "Then compliment her on how nicely she does the dishes. Tell her she smells good. Tell her that her feet are beautiful especially when compared to your big, stinking, furry things."

Ralph's shoulders sagged, but he nodded slowly. "Guess I can try." He shuffled off.

"Didn't it occur to him that you're not married?" Kelly asked, laughing, from beside him.

A shock went through Tough's chest. That was his fear. Kelly hit it.

He shrugged it off. "He was too upset to notice. Wish his wife would appreciate his effort rather than judge him because he doesn't meet her standard."

"You know, she might have complained only once, years ago, but he never forgot."

"True. Men have fragile egos. And they're very protective of them."

Ralph drove away, waving out the window and hollering goodbye. The folks with the food tables followed, leaving Tough and Kelly alone with only the cab light which shone from his open truck door.

Kelly narrowed her eyes and seemed to study him in the light from his cab. "You seem like you know what you're talking about."

Tough's own male pride wanted to shut the conversation down, but he reminded himself that Kelly had trusted him, sweetly and completely, on the tractor. He could try to trust her too. "When you don't talk a lot, sometimes you end up hearing more."

Her lips pursed. She nodded, tapping her lip with her finger. "I can see how that would be true." She shook her head, her blond hair catching the light and rippling over her shoulders. Her teeth flashed. "I had a great time today. Thank you so much." She unzipped his jacket. "Thanks for letting me borrow this."

She moved to shrug it off, and he reached to stop her, meaning to tell her that she might want to keep it because the heater in his truck only worked half the time and he hadn't gotten the time to fix it, would have made time if he'd realized that he'd have Kelly, but she stumbled as she moved forward. His outstretched hand slipped between her waist and the coat.

She froze. The coat fell.

He knew right away he should drop his hand, yank it back, step away. But he didn't.

He moved forward, brought his other hand up, slid them both around her waist, feeling the warmth and the gentle arc of her hips. Pulling her closer, he struggled not to jerk in reaction as he felt her hands slide over his t-shirt, across his sides, and around his back. His whole body shuddered.

She froze. "Cold?"

"Frig, no." He was burning up. On fire. He'd done the friend thing all day. All day, he'd wanted more. More than she could give. Even now, he was pushing for more, the logical part of his brain fighting to be heard over the beating of his heart that wanted to pull her tight and never let her go. His heart asked where the harm was in one little kiss. His head reminded him how very wrong that was.

He swallowed and managed to pull his hands down, resting them in the indentation of her waist, leaning back, putting another fraction of an inch between them. "I'd kill the man who touched you like this when my ring was on your finger."

"I took it off." Her voice floated like a wisp of fog through the air.

His hands tightened. It didn't matter. The promise was still there. He couldn't steal from another man.

He took a shaky breath, searching deep to find the strength to let go, back away. His feet were rooted to the ground, and his hands wouldn't move. He lowered his head. Her breath caught. His mouth hovered just beside her cheek, so close. His body seemed powerless to do anything but move closer.

Where was the flood, the earthquake when he needed it?

At the thought of an earthquake, the story of Achan popped into his head. Achan had taken what wasn't his and hidden it. Eventually, he was found out, and the ground had opened up and swallowed not only him but his whole family.

If he kissed Kelly, no one but she and he need know. They could hide it. It wouldn't make it right.

He dropped his hands and backed away. Her touch slid across his back and over his hips before falling off completely. He closed his eyes against the pain of the aching desire to step back into the circle of her embrace.

Taking another shaky breath, he lifted his cap and ran his hand through his hair. "I'm sorry."

"Don't be. I'm a big girl, and all I had to do was say 'stop.'"

He shoved his ball cap back down on his head. "Why didn't you?"

She stood there, panting in the darkness for a moment before giving a little shrug with her shoulders and bending to pick up his jacket.

He cleared his throat. "You'll want to keep that. I need to fix the heater in my truck."

"You've worn nothing but a t-shirt all day because I have your jacket. It's your turn."

He could be standing buck naked at the South Pole with a blizzard swirling around him, and he wouldn't be cold. Not for a very long time. "I'm not cold. Please keep it."

Placing his hand on the open door, he asked, "Are you ready?"

"Yes." She moved over and jumped in, careful not to touch him, and he supposed he deserved it.

They bounced over the rutted hayfield that had doubled as a parking lot today, in silence. When they pulled onto the road, he forced his tongue to work, hating the awkward silence that threatened to ruin what had been the best day of his life. "A fellow told me there's a little store up here that makes really good pumpkin lattes. Want one?"

Seconds ticked by, and he was afraid she wasn't going to allow his earlier almost-kiss gaffe to slide. Which surprised him because he'd thought Kelly was better than that.

"I do." She turned and smiled at him. The smile gave him hope.

Following the directions that the man had given him earlier, Tough took a right off the main highway and headed uptown. A "For Rent" sign in a warehouse window caught his eyes.

He had never considered moving his garage to a completely different town, but why not? Thoughts of the old men who helped him tempered his consideration, but he tried to be rational. He couldn't help anyone if he didn't have a building. It wouldn't hurt to check, anyway.

He glanced at the sign again before they passed it. The building was perfect, even already had a garage door opening onto the street. He needed to get away from Kelly, anyway. Every second he spent with her made him love her that much more. She was the rare kind of person who got better as one got to know them.

But he had the rest of the evening with her and didn't want to ruin it. How could he get the number without Kelly asking why? He hadn't wanted to ruin their day by telling her about the eviction, and he still wasn't sure he was going to tell her because he didn't want her to feel bad. Maybe he didn't want to move this far away anyway.

Figuring he'd make a decision on the way home, he found the street he needed, and a couple of blocks later, he found Windy Day coffee shop, tucked between a small grocery and a day care center. It was busy, which he figured boded well for their coffee, but he had to park a block away.

"You mind walking?"

"I've ridden on a tractor, used the winch on your tow truck, rode in a weight sled, and even manned the food booth so Joyce could take a bathroom break. A walk down the sidewalk is nothing compared to the rest of that stuff."

They hopped out, and he walked around.

"Now was it that bad?" he asked as he shut her door behind her and started walking beside her down the sidewalk. He wanted to take her hand, even started to. But the almost-kiss had almost turned a great day into a disaster. He couldn't risk it again.

"No. I loved it. How soon do we get to do it again?"

"Depends. I could get called out for a tow anytime. You can come along and use the winch."

She laughed, like he'd hoped she would, and bumped his shoulder. It took a second for him to realize that she'd slipped her hand into his. Volts of electric current shocked up through his arm, and his heart stuttered. He curved his fingers around hers, loving the feeling of connection that cradling her hand brought. He'd meant every word of what he'd said earlier. Not normally a violent man at all, he'd kill the man who touched his woman. But Kelly had taken his hand on her own. That was a little different.

They ordered coffees and a Danish and sat at a little table in the corner talking about their day and the family and nothing and everything. Finally, he checked his phone and realized two hours had gone by and he hadn't even noticed. "It's almost ten. I'd better get you home."

"I can't believe it's that late!" Kelly exclaimed.

He couldn't believe that he was sitting at a little table across from the most amazing, unselfish, beautiful woman in the world. Her cheeks were flushed red, and her blue eyes sparkled from the sun and breeze and a day of fun. Her hair was perfectly windblown and gave her a fresh, youthful, innocent look that a bunch of pretentious fussing would have ruined. But it was her smile, unaffected and easy, her can-do, will-try-it attitude, and her unselfish, giving heart that had stolen his.

The desire to tell her that she had his heart ripped through him, and his mouth opened. He snapped it shut immediately.

She tilted her head and regarded him curiously. "What? What were you going to say?"

"Nothing."

Shaking her head, she laughed. "No. You are not even allowed to go there. Do you remember when we first met how you wouldn't talk to me and wouldn't even look at me?" She looked down at their hands which were threaded together and resting on the table. "Now look at you. You almost smiled twice today."

"I smiled more than that. This was the best day of my life." He stared into her eyes as he said it, meaning every word.

Her brows furrowed. "Really? Didn't you do stuff like this with your family when you were little?"

"No."

"Never?"

"No."

"Tough. You're giving me the silent treatment again." She squeezed his fingers.

"There'd been a lot of sadness—when my dad left, when my mom got sick, when she died." His mother dying had left a deeper hole in his heart than anything else in his life. She was the only other woman he'd ever loved, and he'd lost her.

He took a breath and plunged ahead. "Gram had a lot to support. We couldn't afford much. We made our own fun in the backyard." He watched his thumb rub slowly over her hand.

He thought she shivered, but she held still and waited, giving him time as his eyes jumped and skipped, moving everywhere, looking at anything but hers. Too much. It was too much to talk about things he never talked about with anyone and look her in the eye too.

Finally, after a few beats of silence, he was able to force himself to meet her eyes.

Her smile had slipped; her breathing was slow. Her forehead wrinkled.

He lifted a shoulder. "We had fun. Wherever Turbo is, people are laughing."

"Except Harris, apparently."

He nodded at the truth of those words.

"It really hurt to lose your mom."

"Yeah." He couldn't say more. He'd never talked about it with anyone. He supposed that some people might have turned to drugs or alcohol as they got older to ease the pain. He'd just walled his heart off. He'd promised his mother he wouldn't chase women like his dad anyway.

"She must have had a beautiful heart."

Tough shook off his own hurt. "I was blessed."

Her eyes clouded, and he figured she was remembering her own mother.

"Do you know where she is?" he asked.

They hadn't been talking about her mother, but her thoughts must have gone in the same direction as his because she lifted a shoulder and said, "She died. I was like, twelve, or something."

She said it casually, like it didn't matter, but her hand tightened in his, and he knew it did. Of course it did. It was her mother. No matter that her mother hadn't seemed to care about her.

"If you hadn't hooked me up with Mrs. Fitzsimmons, my life would be a lot different."

He nodded, bringing his other hand up and lightly stroking the fingers he held.

"I was always very aware of that growing up. That I'd been blessed." She also brought her other hand to the table, and somehow, they ended up with both hands twined together.

"Ever since I can remember, I've been on a mission to help other kids like me. In any way I can. That's how Preston and I made our agreement."

He'd forgotten about Preston. Again. He tugged at his hands, but she held on tight.

"Through my work, but also through the charities and the people that I've known through the Fitzsimmons, I've seen people who looked like they were so in love, and I've seen that love die, those people split, their children crying and broken." She stroked his hand with her thumb, and it was all he could do to not close his eyes and moan. It felt so good, so right, but he knew what she was going to tell him before she even finished. Still, he allowed her to talk.

"I decided love was a sham. It didn't last. It never lasted. All that happened was whatever that feeling was that people called love, it made them make foolish decisions, act stupid, then rip their kids' hearts out when they fell out of love with their spouse and fell in love with someone else. I made a vow that I wasn't going to do that. I was going to marry someone I loved, but not in that passionate, can't-see-things-straight way."

Tough waited. He knew what she was saying was wrong. That love did last. The passionate kind of love. Not only had he loved her since the first grade, but he knew people could choose to continue to love. Just like he could choose to let her go. And since that had to be his choice, he couldn't, and wasn't going to, argue with her.

She lifted their clasped hands and ran his fingers against the soft skin of her jaw. He gritted his teeth.

"I understand that feelings come and go. But I've never felt anything this strong. I'm not even sure I understand."

His heart beat painfully. She was killing him. Slowly. So slowly.

He slipped his hand free and turned it so he cupped her cheek, running his thumb over her skin and resting it at the corner of her mouth. So tempting.

"Closing time, you two." A matronly woman in a ruffled pink apron walked by their table. "We've enjoyed watching you guys. You're so in love." She disappeared into the restroom.

Tough stroked his thumb lightly over the corner of her mouth. No. He wasn't going there.

"Let's go." He dropped his hand and stood, legs cramping from being seated so long. He hadn't even realized it'd been hours.

Kelly rose, a bit unsteady too. He put an arm around her, pulled her close, like she was really his, and walked out to his truck.

# Chapter Sixteen

Kelly couldn't believe they'd talked to each other for hours. Especially since Tough wasn't exactly a talker. But she had not monopolized the conversation; she was sure of it. Tough had talked. He'd been witty, funny even, with a dry sense of humor that she loved. Especially when he used that deep, rough tone that threw sparks all through her body.

She felt like she was walking on a cloud when they stepped out of the coffee shop. Reality didn't even intrude when her door handle stuck.

Tough shrugged. "It does this sometimes. I have to take the door apart to fix it. You mind getting in my side?"

He walked her around and opened the driver's door. She slid across the bench seat, working her legs around the gear shifter.

Tough slid in beside her, and she froze. Her whole body was pressed to his, shoulders, hips, and thighs. Her heart raced. She could stay here. Just sit beside him.

His arm slipped behind her, over the back of her seat. He threaded his left hand through the steering column to turn the key. "It'd be warmer if you stay there, since the heater isn't working."

"You don't mind?" It seemed like the back of his teeth were grinding together.

"No. Can't think of too many things I'd like more."

She took one last look at his bunching jaw muscles and mentally shrugged.

"Need me to get your seatbelt?" he asked, his voice rough and low.

"The heater doesn't work, but there's a seatbelt?"

One side of his lips lifted. "It's like I planned this."

She laughed. "One thing I am one hundred percent sure of, you did not plan this." Fumbling beside her, she finally found the belt, but no matter how she twisted, she couldn't get it latched.

"Ugh. Are you sure this actually latches?"

"No. Never used it." He brought his left hand around between them, brushing her hip.

His lips were pressed tight together, and he seemed to be concentrating hard. The belt went together with a metallic *click*.

"Thanks." She gave a little laugh.

He shrugged like it wasn't a big deal and pulled out.

Kelly was jerked out of her happy reverie when he stopped just a few blocks from the coffee shop.

"Be right back," Tough said before he hopped out.

He didn't lie; he was back in less than a minute, stuffing his phone into his pocket.

"What was that about?" she asked.

Staring straight ahead, he didn't answer while he pulled back onto the main road through town, which was much busier than the area they'd just come from despite the late hour. He sighed.

"Are you doing that thing again where you don't talk to me?" she asked, only half-joking.

"No. I'm doing the thing where I'm trying to figure out how not to tell you something."

"Oh. What is it that you don't want to tell me?"

"I got a phone number."

"From the building?"

"Yeah."

Oh, boy. The man could be infuriating. She supposed that if he didn't want to tell her, she didn't have the right to demand an answer. Pressing her lips together, she tried to look straight ahead and pretend she wasn't a little hurt that there was something he knew that he wouldn't tell her.

Ten minutes must have gone by before he spoke. "I noticed a 'For Rent' sign on the way there, and I stopped and got the number because...because I thought it might be a good place to have a garage."

"Oh, that's great. You're going to expand? That's exciting!" She turned smiling eyes on him, but he kept his gaze on the road, one hand on the wheel, the other still resting on the seat behind her. He hadn't touched her, not to put his hand on her shoulder or to pull her closer, and she had to admit she was glad but disappointed as well. She wasn't sure, but she thought she felt him playing with a few strands of her hair. It shifted every so often.

He took the turn for the main highway and never did answer her.

"OH, MY GOSH, OH, MY GOSH." Harris rushed into the warehouse where Kelly and Tough were working early Monday morning, waving her phone in the air.

She saw Tough and froze. Her hand, which had been waving her phone in the air, came down and slid around her back. A flush rose up her cheeks until they matched the color of her hair. "Oh," she said. Kelly almost felt sorry for her. She cleared her throat and lowered her voice an octave, the very picture of a sedate librarian. "Good morning, Tough."

Tough's brows furrowed. He blinked slowly then looked from Kelly back to Harris. He opened his mouth, closed it, then started down the ladder from where he had been installing light fixtures on the ceiling. "I need to, um, to...do something in the shop. I'll just go do...something, now." He turned and, despite the hesitation in his words, strode confidently out of the shop. Kelly watched him go.

"Keeeellllyyyy," Harris hissed.

"You don't have to whisper. He's gone." Kelly laughed.

Instantly Harris's eyes lit back up, and she hopped up and down. Her phone came out from around her back, and she grinned like a child at Christmas. "She answered you! Dr. T has your letter in her column today!"

"No way!" Kelly threw down the window squeegee she had been using and looked frantically around. Where had she laid her phone? She groaned. When she'd come in this morning, she'd walked into Tough's shop and through his office. Since the door always stuck, she'd set her phone on his desk to use two hands to open it and never picked it back up.

"My phone's in Tough's office. What did she say?" Kelly jogged over to Harris and tried to peek over her shoulder at her phone.

"I don't know. As soon as I realized it was your letter, I tried to call you, but you didn't answer. Since you said you'd been working early and late here, I ran over because I just couldn't wait!" Her voice squealed at the end, and she handed her phone to Kelly. "Read it aloud, please."

Kelly put a hand up, refusing to take the phone. "No, you read it."

Harris waved it in her face. "It's your letter."

"But I want her to tell me that..."

"Yeah? You've decided what you want without Dr. T? What did you decide?"

"No. I haven't. I don't know. Read it please."

"Okay, fine." Harris lifted her phone up and cleared her throat dramatically. "Ready?"

Kelly nodded, her stomach tightening into a small ball that seemed to bounce around her chest cavity.

"'Dear Kelly in Brickly Springs—'" Harris looked up. "I still can't believe you used your real name."

Kelly looked at the unfinished ceiling. "I know. That was dumb. Go on."

"'I disagree with you about the staying power of love, but that's not really the issue. I personally put a lot of stock in integrity and character, but that's not really the issue either. You're afraid. Can't blame you. But that's the issue. That, and you're right—fights about money cause about half of the divorces in this country. I have a hunch the poor guy is hiding something. If you can't figure out what, pick the affluent man. That's the safe choice. -Dr. T.'"

Harris allowed her hand to fall slowly to her side. "He's right. I never thought of that. Tough must have a gambling addiction."

Kelly came out of her stupor long enough to snort. "Oh, please. Where in the world did that idea come from?"

"You don't think so?" Harris asked with wide eyes.

"No," Kelly said with conviction, knowing her friend must be joking. But, really, how did she know? Tough didn't spend a lot of time away from the shop, but gambling, especially on the lottery, didn't take much time and... "His shop is busy all the time. He even talked on Saturday night about opening another one."

"Really? Another shop? Where? Across town? That's a great idea."

"No, actually he was looking at a building an hour from here."

"Oh." Harris shrugged. "That seems like stretching it pretty thin. Does he have someone lined up to run one of them?"

Why hadn't she thought about that? "Maybe. I don't know."

"Honestly, Kelly, I think Dr. T has a great point," Harris said thoughtfully. "Tough does work hard. His shop is busy. But he doesn't have a house and drives an old truck around...my mechanic has always cost me big bucks, and his house, which is just a little ways up from his shop, is pretty nice."

"Maybe his wife works?"

"True. Tough only has himself. But he only has to support himself too. And he doesn't spend his money on clothes or vehicles or toys, that's for sure."

Kelly crossed her arms and tapped her nose, trying to figure out if Dr. T had a valid point. Was Tough hiding something? Like a hidden addiction? She could hardly believe it. He had more self-control than she did. "I don't think Dr. T was saying to choose money... I think he was saying 'make sure you know the guy.'"

Harris nodded. "I definitely think there was a hidden meaning in there. It's almost like he knows Tough, because Tough is quiet, but I think there's a lot going on in that brain of his."

Kelly knew that to be true, without a doubt. Preston was nice, but he often tried to make himself look better than he was. Tough was...the opposite.

"I can't stay. I need to get across town to the library."

"Yeah. I know. Thanks so much for coming over with the news. She took so long to answer that I quit looking."

"You mean you spent the weekend with Tough and didn't think about anything else?" Harris laughed as she fixed her purse strap and walked to the door. "Call me later."

"Sure," Kelly said.

Kelly took a moment to admire how close the work was to being completed. She might even be able to open up next week. Possibly. If she had enough volunteer staff to start out with.

She turned and walked back down the short hall to the door between her side and Tough's. Better get her phone before she started washing windows again. Otherwise she'd end up working too long and being late for her real job.

Shoving the door, she was able to get it open the first time, and she stepped through into Tough's office. Actually, she really had to hold herself back, because if Tough gambled or had some other major issue, a quick look at his books would surely show it. But if someone were to go into her home and root through her stuff...if *Tough* were to go into her home and root, it would upset her. She would wonder why didn't he just ask.

That's what she'd do. She'd simply ask Tough if he had a gambling problem. Even as she thought it, she knew it wasn't true. There was no way.

Her phone lay on the corner of his desk beside his mouse pad. She grabbed it, bumping his mouse in the process. The screensaver blinked and disappeared. Kelly stared at his screen. A mostly clear desktop with an accounting software icon and an icon for the internet. That was it.

Holding her phone tightly, she moved through to the shop. Her car was parked on the other side, and it was almost time for her to go.

Tough bought groceries for that lady and donated his time at the truck pull. Maybe he gave most of his money away? No. She couldn't believe that. People donated, she'd seen it with her own eyes, but never at the expense of a house or nice car for themselves.

She shook her head. That didn't make sense either. Honestly, it seemed to her that Dr. T had been telling her, in a roundabout way, but still telling her, that she should pick Preston. Dr. T probably knew what he was talking about. It's why she wrote to him.

Tough leaned against the hood of an old, golden brown car while a little old lady clutched her hands like she was driving a car and seemed to be telling him there was something wrong with the steering. Tough nodded and listened intently. But his eyes jerked up as Kelly walked in front of him toward the door.

The lady stopped talking.

Kelly smiled at the lady before facing Tough. "I'll be back after work. Thanks for your help."

His eyes lit, and he nodded, watching until she turned and continued to walk to the door. She waved to Al and Mr. Sigel before she walked out.

# Chapter Seventeen



*Two weeks later*

Kelly waited in the airport terminal. Anxious. Eager. Afraid. All those emotions churned in her stomach like cement in a mixer. She'd never said anything to Preston. Partly because service was so spotty and their times were all mixed up. Plus, it wasn't like they were constantly calling and talking to each other at a normal time. If nothing else, this trip really made her see that what she felt for Preston was not nearly as powerful as her feelings for Tough.

She rubbed her purse strap. There really was more. Whatever the feeling could be. She didn't feel for Preston what she felt for Tough. Didn't long to talk to him all the time, didn't long to touch him, to see him, even to just catch a whiff of his scent. Nothing like that at all.

The board flashed. His flight was docked and unloading. She looked around, trying to push thoughts of Tough out of her head. She needed to focus on dealing with Preston first.

Lifting her phone, she checked for a text. When she looked up, he was walking toward her, his sandy hair falling over his forehead, looking pressed and fresh despite the long flight. He pulled a large suitcase beside him, and his leather shoulder bag was slung over his shoulder.

"Hey!" Kelly stood and walked over to meet him.

He smiled at her. A friendly smile. His green eyes didn't hesitate to meet hers. There were no secrets in them. They didn't compel her to move toward him, or to touch him, or...

"Hey! So nice of you to pick me up." He reached her, grabbing her shoulders and kissing her cheek. The same greeting he gave her whether they'd been across the room from each other for an evening charity gala or, apparently, separated for two weeks with an ocean between them. But that wasn't a fair assessment, since her heart and soul was not longing for him. The friendly peck on the cheek was more than enough.

He stepped back. "Want to grab a bite to eat? I'm fried, but I'm hungry, too. I'd love some good food."

"I'd love to. I know just the place." The same little mom-and-pop store and restaurant that Tough had taken her to. "Can you wait thirty minutes?"

"I can. But no more."

His phone dinged, and she glanced at it as he took it out of his pocket. He tilted it away from her, almost like he didn't want her to see it. Odd. She looked up at his face. He read the text without expression.

Maybe the light was glaring on his phone.

They walked to the car and loaded his stuff. He was content to sit in the passenger seat and talk about his trip.

She listened, commenting, realizing this was the same kind of thing they'd always talked about. They'd fallen into the easy business-like relationship she'd grown used to. It didn't bother her at all except to wonder was this what she wanted for her marriage? Did she want a casual peck on the cheek? Was he attracted to her just a little? She'd thought they loved each other. Maybe he really did love her. Wouldn't he want to kiss her, at least?

Luckily there was a spot along the street in front of Pop's, and she grabbed it.

"Really, Kelly?" Preston looked at the dinky store, and she saw it from his eyes. Dirty. Small. Cheap.

"The food is so amazing. I really wanted you to try it."

He sighed, put out, and she couldn't believe she'd made such a huge blunder. What had she been thinking? This wasn't Preston's idea of "good food."

"I'm sorry. I just found this place. It's close to where my newest activity center is, and I loved it. I wanted to share. Obviously, I wasn't thinking straight, or I would have realized it wasn't something you would enjoy." She bit her lip and rubbed her hand over the steering wheel. "We can go somewhere else?" She loved the place. Because it was in such a rough part of town, she felt they needed the business. If Preston liked it, he'd refer his friends...

"No." He reached for the door handle. "We're here now. I can make do. Plus, if you say it's good, I'm sure it is. You have impeccable taste."

They got out and walked in. Kelly stood back and allowed Preston to pick the seat. She was thankful when he chose one right by the window. Not that she enjoyed the passersby on the sidewalks being able to look in at them, but more because the table in the back, where they were mostly obscured, where she and Tough had eaten, was special. Sacred, maybe, and she didn't want to sit there with Preston.

Preston scanned the menu. "So what did you have that was so good?"

"Well, their Greek food is authentic. The salad was amazing, but the gyro looked really good, and I think you'd like it."

"So you've been here multiple times?" he asked without looking up.

"Nope. Just once."

"Who were you with?" He laid the menu down and looked over the table at her.

"A friend. One who was helping me with the activity center."

"Cassidy? Harris?"

"Tough Baxter. You don't know him."

"Tough? That's an actual name? Were his parents drunk or high when they named him?"

She shrugged, ignoring his rudeness. She'd heard much stranger names. "His whole family has odd names. Some people do that." She tapped her menu. "When you figure out what you want, we have to go up and order it ourselves."

"Really?" Preston looked around. "There's no server?"

"Nope." Kelly smiled, but Preston's mouth flattened. "I can order for you if you want."

"Yeah. Do that, please. I'm tired. I'll take the gyro if you think that's what I'll like."

She went up, placed their order, and paid for it, bringing their drinks back with her.

"No alcohol?"

She shook her head. "They don't serve it here."

Was this a good time to broach the serious conversations she wanted to have? He was tired and grumpy from his flight and trip. But she didn't want to wait. Every day that she procrastinated was one more day that she'd stolen from Preston being able to move forward.

Funny how she was so comfortable talking to him about his business details and things that no one else but Preston and she knew in politics, charities, and his attorney practice, but it dawned on her that they really didn't have personal conversations.

His phone dinged again with yet another text. It had been almost constant since she'd picked him up. And he kept holding his phone so it slanted away from her.

She opened her mouth to ask him who it was. The clerk, a different one than the last time she was here with Tough, brought their food. Preston waited until she left then picked up his fork. "What's up? Something's on your mind."

"I'm not sure," Kelly said slowly. A thought, one of those random, "the universe just dropped it in my head" kind of thoughts, just popped into her head. She considered her next question carefully because she knew it could change her life. "Where...where do you meet your girlfriend?"

"I'm very discreet, you know that, Kelly. Why?" He paused with his fork halfway to his mouth. "Did you hear something? Surely not."

"No. No, I didn't hear anything." She spoke, but her words felt cut off. Distant. Like they came out of someone else's mouth while she watched from a very high mountain. She wasn't hurt, just shocked. This was not something that she'd expected or thought. Preston didn't realize he'd dealt her such a severe blow.

He swallowed, all but smacking his lips. "You're right. This is amazing. The best gyro I've ever had."

"The shop owners are from Greece." Her mouth worked. The right words came out. But she felt like she was having an out-of-body experience.

Preston was acting like...like he thought she knew. Or should have known.

She thought she loved him. She just figured...figured what? That Preston wasn't demonstrative? That they were so comfortable with each other since they practically grew up together? She had never considered their lack of passion. Not until Tough.

Had Preston taken their lack for granted? Like he knew, and she knew, they just made a good couple? Her chest felt frozen. But it didn't hurt. Not really. She wasn't devastated. Not like she would be if Tough...

A shadow fell over the table. Tough stood there in a white tee, old jeans, and work boots, holding his used plate and balled-up napkin. He must have been eating at the table where they'd sat together. A pang went through her at the thought of him eating alone. As usual.

His eyes, dark and deep, studied her, asking questions she couldn't answer, demanding answers she couldn't give, offering support she could never accept.

She took a breath. "Tough." Her voice was an octave too high with too much tremolo. Clearing her throat, she slapped a smile on her face. "Preston, this is Tough Baxter. I told you he was helping me renovate?"

"You did."

Tough didn't offer his hand, and neither did Preston, who also didn't stand up.

Preston looked at her. "Is this the activity center I specifically told you I didn't want you to do until our wedding was planned?"

"It is."

Preston's lips pinched together. "I see." He chewed thoughtfully then swallowed. "We need to talk about the wedding." He looked over at Tough as though surprised to see him still there. "Did you need something?" Preston asked, his tone haughty.

Kelly set her unused fork down and stood, pushing the rush of anger that swamped the back of her neck down. She refused to allow him to make her angry. "I actually wanted to talk to Tough for a few minutes, if you'll excuse me."

She took Tough's arm and dragged him out the door behind her where they could talk on the sidewalk.

But she didn't have anything to say. Not really. She just needed to recover from the shock that shouldn't have been a shock. And to allow the unexpected anger to fade.

She ended up standing on the sidewalk, facing Tough, her hand still on his arm. His eyes still asking the questions she wouldn't answer.

A deep sigh slipped out from between her lips. "I didn't know. I mean, I thought we loved each other. I knew we were friends. We both wanted to make his mom happy, but I didn't know he was planning...that he..." She ran a hand through her hair. "I didn't know."

"Stop." Tough's voice came out, low, deep, commanding. "He doesn't know. He doesn't know what is sitting right across from him." He raised a finger and touched the corner of her lip. "You're beautiful. More beautiful than you usually are. He didn't even notice that you dressed for him, you fixed your hair for him and put on this for him." He tapped her cheek with his hand, indicating her makeup.

He was right. She had done a little extra to meet Preston. And he hadn't noticed. "Does it matter? Did I know it all along?" Why was she asking Tough anyway? Maybe because he inserted himself into their discussion. Only because she had allowed it. At least the anger that had been strangling her throat had dissipated somewhat.

"I guess it depends on what you want." He crossed his arms over his chest and looked over her head.

She pulled both lips in. "I thought I knew what I wanted. I really did. But I'm not sure anymore."

"You deserve all his money and all the things that it can buy. You deserve to be able to help all the kids you want, to do the good that you need to do. This world needs you. Up until I heard him today, I thought the price was worth it." He shifted and hung a hand behind his neck. "Now I'm not sure."

Her mind snapped into place. "I've known for a while what I need to do." She started to moved toward the door, but Tough placed a light hand on her arm.

"Are you sure?"

She looked up, surprised he'd question her. Didn't he just say that she should dump the jerk? "Yes. I know exactly what I'm doing. My eyes are completely open."

Tough's pressed lips and tense posture said that he wasn't sure, but he didn't argue. He opened his mouth as though to say one last thing but ended up closing it and nodding. "You're sure?"

"Yes."

"I'm here if you need me."

She nodded then made her way back into the restaurant and to Preston who had finished his gyro.

"Would you like me to order you dessert?"

"Is it good?" Preston asked like he hadn't just told her he had a girlfriend on the side. Like she hadn't just walked out and had a personal conversation with another man. The tightness gripped her throat again, and she pushed it away.

"It is. I know exactly what you'll like." She ordered the baklava and carried it over to their table, setting it down in front of him.

She took her seat in front of her untouched meal. "Do you stick with just one girl, or do your girlfriends come and go?" Why couldn't she let it go? She was breaking up with him. But the questions just kept tumbling out of her mouth, and with each of his innocent answers, she got the confirmation she needed. If she ever doubted this was the right decision, he had confirmed it over and over again. How had they gotten such different ideas of what their relationship was going to look like?

"I've had the same one since we were freshmen in high school." Another punch in the gut. He'd been with her for over twelve years. The whole time they'd casually, then not so casually, talked about joining forces, making his mother happy. Sure, they weren't really passionate, but she'd thought she loved him—she'd been focused on saving every child she could, paying her debt to society, really. But she supposed if he'd had casual hookups...but the same girl for twelve years? Why had he even led Kelly on? Got engaged to her?

She tried not to allow her face to show her shock and pain. "Why don't you just marry her?"

He rolled his eyes. "It's Bonita, Kelly. I can't marry her."

Bonita. The daughter of their long-time housekeeper. As far as Kelly knew, she'd never seen a dad. Bonita.

"Because she's Hispanic?" The anger threatened again, and she almost let it loose.

"No. That's an asset, really. But...she's not you. She couldn't organize a fundraiser, or host a Christmas party for my law practice, or know what to say or do when we're out together. She doesn't have your class, your drive, she's just..."

"Good in the sack."

"Of course." Preston almost rolled his eyes. Kelly couldn't believe he couldn't see the steam coming out of her ears. For Bonita and for herself. That he would casually dismiss Bonita, who maybe didn't go to college but had a respectable job as manager of the convenience store about a mile from Preston's mansion. And who was more than capable of doing what Kelly did if Preston would take the time to teach her.

"What does she think of us?"

"She hates it." He shrugged. "But it's not like you and I—" He waved a hand in the air.

Yeah. They weren't physical. And now she knew why.

Sure, their relationship had never had passion. She had been content with a platonic friendship, thinking that when they got married... Or that... The steam went right out of her sails. She hadn't even thought about how Preston felt about it. She'd been as focused on her career and as satisfied as him with the status of their relationship. It wasn't until Tough came into her life that she even considered that she might be missing something. Still, she hadn't gotten past the hurdle of love lasting. If that's even what she felt.

She brought a cleansing breath into her lungs and blew it out.

She opened her mouth and spit it out. "I think we ought to reconsider our engagement."

Preston didn't even look up. "I told you that's fine. You want more? What can I do for you?"

"No. I want out."

He finally put his fork down and stared at her. "Seriously?"

"Yes."

His jaw tightened. "What about Mom?"

"I think your mom will want us to be happy. I can't imagine she would want me to feel like I'm making a huge mistake. I know she wouldn't want you married to me but in love—" She cringed inside over the words. Was it real? "—in love with Bonita."

He put a hand up, and his face relaxed, though he still didn't look happy. And rightfully so. "You're right. The nondisclosure still holds, but...are you sure? This is really going to throw a wrench into my plans."

She fiddled with the edge of the tablecloth. "I think it's best to do it now. I did not move forward on the wedding, so no one will know it's called off."

Preston got a thoughtful look on his face. "Do you know of anyone else who could take your place?"

She blew out. "Honestly, Preston, I've been wondering for a while if there was more to our relationship, but the girlfriend thing... I think you should marry Bonita. You must love her if you've spent the last twelve years with her. She must love you, for that matter."

"I've been completely faithful to her. What's not to love?" His face lost its tightness, and his eyes seemed to glow as he talked about her.

"Marry her, for goodness' sake."

"What will everyone say? Holy smokes. What will everyone think?"

"If you love her, it shouldn't matter." Kelly found that she might actually believe those words as they came out.

Preston twiddled his fork. "The reality is she doesn't have the confidence to do what you do. I had to have someone who could do all the stuff that she didn't want to do."

That burned. Kelly tried not to take it personally. After all, she had been spending the last few weeks running around with Tough, having thoughts that an engaged woman had no business having. She'd never been tempted before, and she suspected she'd never be tempted again, but...

"This whole conversation is kind of a shock to me."

He steepled his fingers. "I see." Tapping the tips of his fingers together, he studied her. "So, would you consider..."

"No. You and Bonita will just have to work that out. Hire someone to be me if you need to."

He sighed deeply, studying his hands. "Photo ops, plane rides, overseas trips, hosting parties, meet and greet, she doesn't want to do any of it."

Kelly kicked her wounded pride to the curb. None of this should be such a surprise. She pulled on her game face. "Do you want me to talk to her? I'd be more than happy to help her out. You know, now that I think about it...Bonita... Your mom would be happy to hear this too."

He grimaced. "I was a little concerned about that. Do you think so?"

Kelly's natural optimism bubbled to the surface. "I'm sure of it. Rather than us getting married, she'll have Bonita be part of the family. I know she'll love that."

"She'll still love you. She'll always love you."

A little sadness pierced her heart as the life she thought she was going to have slipped away forever. "I know."

"Well..." He stood. "I guess this is goodbye for now."

She stood with him, gathering up her uneaten food. Her equilibrium had returned, but her world did not look the same now as it had when she walked in. She wasn't sure what she was going to do about it. First thing...man, she didn't even know what the first thing was.

"Hey, Kelly?"

"Yeah?"

"I'm not going to just drop your charities." Preston gave her a hesitant smile.

"I know. I didn't think you would." She pulled the ring out of her purse. The widening of his eyes and his dropped jaw said that he hadn't even noticed she wasn't wearing it. "I suppose I should give you this back."

He waved a hand. "Nah. Keep it. Bonita won't want it anyway. Too big and pretentious."

Kelly pressed her lips together. What had made him think she wanted a big, pretentious ring? She needed to calm down.

With her mind jumbled and fear peeking its dark head over her shoulder, she moved to lead Preston out of the restaurant. "Do you want me to just drop you off at Bonita's house?"

He looked a little sheepish. "She'll be waiting in my room at my house."

Kelly had never been in his room. She'd never *wanted* to be in his room. Maybe he knew her better than she thought. With a shake of her head and a small eye roll at her own stupidity, she walked out.

# Chapter Eighteen

Kelly lifted Nessa, who had gotten tired of listening to Harris read a story to the other children at the activity center, and set her onto her hip. "We should have kept the kids so you and Torque could go on a real honeymoon."

Cassidy shrugged, picking up a stray ball that had rolled over to the small kitchenette from the basketball court. "It's kind of crazy, but we do have a nanny to help part-time. I pay her for full-time so we can escape in the evening after the kids are in bed." She blushed. "It's been nice."

Happiness for her friend filled Kelly's chest with warmth. "I'm so glad things worked out for Torque and you."

"I never, not in a million years, thought they would." Cassidy leaned down and picked up Nissa who was pulling on her skirt. "But sometimes life gives you blessings you don't deserve."

"True." And sometimes it gave you exactly what you deserved. Kelly tried not to fall into negative thinking. Her activity center was almost ready to go. The gym floor wouldn't be put down since it was a specialized thing that even Tough didn't want to try to attempt. It was going to be expensive, but at least everything else was almost done.

"Isn't Preston supposed to get home soon?" Cassidy asked as Nissa tried to pull her earring out.

Kelly cringed inside. She straightened her shoulders and said as casually as possible, "He's back."

"Oh." Cassidy gave Kelly a considering look. "I know you weren't sure about him, but he's been out of the country for weeks..."

"We broke up." Nessa wiggled. Kelly set her down on the activity room floor and watched as she toddled over to the reading circle.

Cassidy blinked like a board had landed in her eye. "Do you need a lawyer to get you out of the contract he made you sign?"

"No." There had been a prenup, but it had been to protect her, not hurt her. The hurt came from another area. She couldn't go into the fact that Preston had had a girlfriend on the side since ninth grade. But it definitely made her feel much less guilty for every second she'd spent with Tough.

Cassidy set Nissa down. She immediately began to cry and fuss to be held, but Cassidy touched Kelly's arm gently. "What are you going to do?"

Kelly bit her lip and blinked back the sudden spring of tears. She wasn't sad about losing Preston. It was more the loss of her security. Or maybe the onset of fear. "I feel like my life is lying around me in ashes."

Cassidy wrapped her arms around Kelly. "At least you didn't get burned." She squeezed tighter. "I know this is something you're still working through, but I think it's because you didn't really love him. Not the way a woman should love her man."

Kelly couldn't argue. If Tough had done to her what Preston did... She and Tough weren't even together, and when he'd ridden with Dusty on her bike, it had felt like Kelly's chest was being torn apart.

Now, Kelly was sad and scared, maybe, feeling the traces of anger, perhaps, but not hurt. Definitely not burned.

Cassidy held her for a minute then leaned back. "We could have a girls' night. You know Harris is always up for it."

The idea was tempting. But she'd always found that staying busy helped her much more than wallowing. Getting together to chat and have fun was one thing. Getting together for everyone to talk about what a massive cave-in her life had become was not appealing at all. At all.

She needed to be occupied. "No. I've got to find something constructive to do."

"Did you tell Tough?" Cassidy asked softly.

"No."

"I think he'd like to know."

Harris stepped over and observed their drawn expressions. "You guys heard too?"

"Heard what?" Cassidy asked.

"Dr. T has decided to unmask herself."

"That's good news, isn't it?" Cassidy asked carefully. Harris was kind of particular when it came to Dr. T.

Harris shook her head emphatically. "No! That's all the fun of it. No one knows who she is."

"Oh."

Kelly thought about the advice Dr. T had given her. It really hadn't helped. "When is she going to unmask herself?"

"She's going to do it in person." Harris sat down on a barstool and put her elbows on the counter, resting her head in her hands.

"Really?" Kelly asked in surprise. She could really see Harris travelling hours to see it.

"Yep."

"Well, where? When?" Cassidy asked.

"She's going to announce that tomorrow on her advice blog that started it all."

"Oh." Kelly grunted. "Probably in California or something."

"She said she was going to do it in her hometown. Of course, no one knows where that is." Harris twisted an earring. "She's going to tell us that tomorrow too. Probably waiting until the last minute so she doesn't get mobbed at whatever venue she's at."

"Well, that's something to look forward to," Cassidy said in a tone that sounded more like a question.

"You seem down." Harris's serious eyes studied Kelly. "What's wrong?"

Kelly hesitated.

Cassidy answered for her, picking Nissa up along with a sippy cup. "She broke up with Preston."

"You want a girls' night? I'm free," Harris asked.

"No, I need to do something more than sitting around. I couldn't sit still anyway." Just look at her tonight. Pacing. "Too bad the activity center is completely finished except for the gym floor, which I can't do." She sighed. "I need to go find something to do." She shifted Nessa. "I'll help you get the twins in the car."

"I'll round up Jamal for you," Harris said and started off.

Kelly and Cassidy chatted as they walked out. While Kelly was waiting for Cassidy to unlock the car, her phone rang. She pulled it out but almost didn't answer it. Her ex-mother-in-law-to-be. They had a great relationship—so close to mother-daughter—that Kelly felt would continue even though Preston and she were no longer getting married, but she wasn't completely sure about that. There was always that doubt since she wasn't really a real part of the family. They'd never adopted her, but she'd lived with them, and they'd paid for her private high school.

"Hello?" she said, shifting Nessa higher on her hip.

"Kelly." Mrs. Fitzsimmons's cultured voice came over the phone. "I just spoke with Preston."

She knew it, but her heart still shivered anyway. "He told you?"

"That you two broke up? Yes," she said matter-of-factly. Her tone softened. "Are you okay?"

Her concern warmed Kelly's heart. "I'm disappointed and not sure what I'm going to do, but emotionally, yes, I'm fine." She blew a breath out. "When Preston was gone, I met someone, and I had a hard time remembering I was engaged. Preston deserves better."

"I'm glad to hear you're fine but less happy to know that you'll be potentially joining another lucky family. You'll have to tell me all about it. Do we know them?"

"Uh, not really," Kelly hedged. She never should have worried about Mrs. Fitzsimmons. She was the same classy lady she'd always been, and she loved Kelly like her own daughter.

Bless her heart, Mrs. Fitzsimmons let it go. "You do know that you are always welcome here. No matter what."

She had thought so. "It's good to hear the reassurance." She relinquished Nessa as Cassidy lifted her out of Kelly's arms.

Mrs. Fitzsimmons seemed to hesitate for a moment before she said, "I, well, I have a favor to ask. I actually thought this might be a good thing for you."

She paused, but before Kelly could say anything, she continued, "I understand you might be looking for some other ways to fund your charities. This afternoon, I got a call from the guest speaker for tomorrow night's black-tie gala in Mansion Heights. Her husband went to the hospital this morning with pain in his stomach and is having emergency gall bladder surgery tomorrow. She won't be able to make the gala. I thought you might be willing to fill in? The people are going to want to hear about Helping Hearts Charity, and you can do that, since you're so intimately involved, but I thought you also might be able to give a few plugs for the things you're doing now. You know, now that Preston is out of the picture. I just thought you might be... rebuilding."

Tears pricked Kelly's eyes again. Mrs. Fitzsimmons had always been so good to her. And there was no doubt in her mind where she'd learned resilience. It wasn't coincidence that Mrs. Fitzsimmons was calling her now, when she knew that Kelly would be down.

"I love you. Thank you so much."

"I love you, too, Kelly. Maybe we need to go shopping for an outfit? Would you be able to take an afternoon off work?"

"I'd love to."

They made a time to meet, and Kelly hung up.

"Good news?" Cassidy asked.

"Yep. I have something to do." Kelly looked around. While she'd been on the phone, Harris had come out with Jamal and they were strapped in the car. Kelly hadn't even noticed. She shook her head. "The keynote cancelled at tomorrow's charity at Mansion Heights, so Preston's mom asked me to fill in."

"So you're speechwriting tonight?" Harris asked. "That's great. You need help?"

"Nah. I'm basically talking about what I do all day. I'll want to jot some notes down so I don't ramble, but it'll be easy."

"All right. Well, I'd better get going before the kids figure out how to get out of their seatbelts," Cassidy said with a wry grin.

"A very real possibility the longer they hang around their dad," Harris said with a grin of her own.

At the mention of Torque, Kelly thought immediately about Tough. "I'm out of here, too," she said, digging her phone out of her purse and pulling up the texting app. Her friends were right. It wouldn't hurt to let him know.

> I talked to Preston today. We ended everything. I just wanted you to know.

She hit send. Not that she was expecting him to come rushing to her side. Not that she expected anything out of him. She was simply letting him know, because maybe, just maybe, he would want to.

She walked to her car and got in. He hadn't texted back. Maybe he was under a car or painting or... She shoved thoughts of Tough aside and started her car.

As she drove home, she thought about the salient points she wanted to make in her speech, not only about the charity for whom she worked, but also about the work she was doing on the side. She'd need a foundation or some kind of tax-exempt way of channeling the money. She seemed to recall Colton, from Cassidy and Torque's wedding, was an accountant. Maybe he could help. Tomorrow she'd ask Cassidy for his number.

Until the donations started coming in, though, she'd need to figure out a way to make enough money to finish the renovations and fund the activity center.

She hadn't figured anything out until she'd gotten home, showered, and sat in front of the fireplace, scratching down a rough outline for her speech. She'd given plenty of speeches in her lifetime, and this one didn't worry her.

It was just after eight when someone knocked at her door. Her outline was done; she had just been fleshing it out some. She set the papers aside and stretched, looking at the clock. Who in the world would be visiting at this hour on a weeknight?

She opened the door. Tough stood on her stoop. His hair was still damp. He smelled like soap and aftershave. Despite the chill, he carried his coat in one hand and wore a collared, short-sleeved button-up shirt tucked into what looked like new jeans. And those cowboy boots.

Her heart drummed in her chest. She put a hand over her rioting stomach and opened the door wider. "Come in. It's cold out."

"Can you step out for a minute?" he asked.

"Let me get a jacket," she said.

He held up the one she'd worn the night of the truck pull. She took it, stepping outside and closing the door behind her. His face gave nothing of his thoughts away, but the way he was dressed made her think he was going on a trip. Or visiting someone in the hospital. Heck, she had no idea. She'd never seen him look so nice, except for the tux, but that was a wedding and...

He took a deep breath, and he looked down into her eyes. "I got your text."

"Good." She nodded and twisted the sleeve of his jacket.

"You gave the ring back?" he asked. He glanced down at her hands as though checking, but her fingers were hidden under the too-long sleeves.

She shook her head, and his eyes clouded. "He wouldn't take it."

"Oh."

"I'm gonna hock it."

His teeth flashed white for just a second. "I might be able to help you with that."

"Figured you could." She shifted and twisted his sleeve the other way. "Is that why you came the whole way over here? To make sure I gave his ring back?"

"No." He stared into her eyes but didn't say anything more. His chest rose and fell like he'd run the whole way here. It matched her own inability to get enough oxygen into her lungs for some reason.

"Then...?"

He put a hand up, in a give-me-a-moment gesture, but instead of letting it fall back down, he moved closer and slid it over her cheek, cupping the back of her neck. "Kelly, I..."

His other hand came up, and he moved closer, their breath mingling. She lifted her own hands, moving them around his back, feeling the hard hotness under his shirt, the play of muscles as he moved his hands in her hair, the thump of his heart which beat almost violently against his ribs.

"I should have told you..." he began in a whisper. But his head leaned down, and he stopped talking as he kissed her forehead, the bridge of her nose, her cheeks.

Her knees trembled, and her fingers gripped his back. He lowered his hands, running them down her back and pulling her against him. Supporting her.

Feelings of warmth and safety mingled with the burning fire that spread from her chest through her belly, and she pushed closer still.

His lips hovered over hers, so close she could almost feel them. "I want to kiss you." He closed his eyes. "I came here to..."

She lifted her head. Their lips touched. Shock waves crashed through her body, and suddenly as close as they were, it wasn't enough. He must have felt it too, because he pushed closer, bending his knees, pressing his lips to hers. Sparks danced behind her eyes as she felt his tongue touch her lips. Then, suddenly, they were closer, and she was hot, then cold, and couldn't think beyond the man in front of her, tasting him, touching him, being closer, wanting more.

A dog barked down the street. He lifted his head, panting. His eyes were slower to open; they lay at half-mast, roaming over her face.

"Can I say that was better than I ever thought it would be?" he asked, his voice husky and raw.

"I'm stunned, myself," she said between pants.

"I've wanted to do that since I was about five."

"I'm glad you waited. I'm still not sure I'm going to survive, and I wouldn't have wanted to die young."

He grinned, still close. His voice sent shivers down her spine. "You're still young."

"Is that what you came for?" she asked, smiling. Wishing he would kiss her again.

He laughed. The sound thrilled her soul. "No. Although if I'd known that was going to happen..." He laughed again. "Actually, I was definitely hoping it would happen."

She raised her brows, hardly daring to believe it. "You came here planning on kissing me?"

His smile disappeared. "No. I came here planning on telling you something I should have told you Saturday, but I didn't want to ruin our day."

Her neck hairs pricked. "Are you going somewhere?"

"Not now."

She glanced at his clothes. "You're all dressed up."

"I had to talk to you, and I wanted to wear something nice. Nicer." He lifted a shoulder like it was no big deal.

"You look good. I love the boots." She couldn't stop her eyes from giving him another slow once-over.

His lips twitched, but then his face grew serious again. His hands, still around her back, rubbed up and down softly. "Mr. Millard came to see me last week. He's selling the building, and he's got a buyer already lined up." Kelly gasped, but Tough kept talking. "The buyer only wants half, so I told him I could be out whenever the buyer closed. If all the paperwork goes through, they're closing the day after tomorrow."

"That's why you were getting a phone number Saturday night." She looked away, at the streetlights that lined the quiet street in front of her house. Was he saying he was leaving? Moving? Her heart slowed into painful thumps.

"Yeah."

"So...you're really leaving?" She didn't really want to hear the answer.

"Yes. I called the number, and I'm driving there now to take him a check to hold the place."

Her world reeled around her, like the bottom had fallen out and she was falling. Her hands gripped Tough, the only solid thing in her universe. She forced her lips to move. "I see."

He took a deep breath, and his hands tightened on her back. He closed his eyes, and his hands unclenched. "That's not really what I came here to say, either."

"Oh?" Hope blossomed in her chest. He was going to stay after all?

Seconds ticked by. A garbage can rattled. The trees shivered as a cool breeze blew across the yard. A few late-season oak leaves drifted slowly down in the porch light. Kelly waited, hardly daring to breathe.

A few drops of sweat glistened on Tough's forehead before he finally opened his mouth. "Kelly, you've got to know how I feel about you. It's not like I've hidden it. I know love scares you. Honestly, it scares me too. The only woman I ever loved died."

His face twisted, and her heart clenched. His mother's death had marked him deeply.

His eyes skimmed away before he forced them back to look at her. "So telling you I love you doesn't mean much to you. But I do. I love you. Maybe it will help you some to realize that I've loved you since I was five. There's some staying power there. It's not a lifetime, but sixty years from now, it will be. I'll love you then, too."

"I—"

He held his hand up. Kelly closed her mouth and waited, her heart feeling like a bumper car in her chest. He slipped the hand back around her waist before continuing.

"I can't give you what you want. Not like Preston could. There's no way I can even come close to that level. I'm not sure I can even give you what you need."

He cleared his throat and swallowed. "I'm going to lose customers with this move, but I scoured the internet last night to try to find a closer place. There's no other property. I don't have a choice, and I don't know when the garage will be successful again. It takes time to build a business and earn the trust of people. Plus, my other...well, the gig is up."

She wasn't sure what he meant, but she couldn't ask. Not now. She held his cheeks in her hands, just a little stubble roughing her skin. He closed his eyes and placed his hands over hers.

"I want you," he whispered roughly. "I want you so bad. But I've just lost everything I've built, and I would never ask you to give up everything. I couldn't."

"Tough, I would..." Kelly's words trailed off, because she realized she was just about to do what she'd derided other people for doing. She had been going to tell him she'd give everything up, her job, her charities, the activity center that she'd just opened, give it all up and go with him to help him start his business over. That she'd do anything as long as it meant not losing him. Was she crazy? She knew people acted like this. They called it love, and they looked so happy together. Then twenty years down the road, heck, five years down the road, they decided they'd grown apart, or fallen out of love, or just didn't have anything in common anymore, or the one she particularly hated, *I never loved you in the first place.* No. She wasn't doing that, wasn't going there.

She couldn't move an hour away. Her job and her charities and the kids she helped were here. From the time she got up in the morning until she went to bed at night.

It would be worth it to give up even a little for Tough. But there she went, giving up everything she'd built for him.

She cleared her throat, which had somehow closed so tightly she strained to breathe. The crushing pain in her chest didn't help either. "Tough, I would really like it if you would kiss me again before you go."

The pain in his eyes flickered, and Kelly's throat tightened even more.

His teeth flashed. He didn't answer her. He didn't need to. Her hands moved around his back as his broad shoulders lowered and his lips claimed hers again. The same full-on, wild shaking of her soul hit her again, and she ended up clinging to Tough as her whole body fought to get closer. His muscles bunched as though trying to pull back, but their lips clung, small kisses, then deep. Her world spun and tilted, until Tough jerked away, stumbling backward down her steps. He caught himself at the bottom, his hands on his knees, his head down.

She leaned back against her wall, her hand on the banister, trying to make her lungs function, to make her legs quit shaking. One hand touched her lips, which still tingled.

Neither of them said anything as the minutes ticked by. Finally, Tough straightened. His eyes were flat brown. Like brown crayon in a little child's picture. His face looked ravaged, as though he'd just watched his best friend walk the gauntlet. He swallowed. "I love you, Kelly. It's not gonna change." He turned. The confident walk she'd always admired, gone. The broad shoulders slumped. The capable hands hanging limp at his side. They were pink and scabbed.

It was the hands that did it. She choked, shoving her fist in her mouth to keep from sobbing out loud, turning and fumbling for the doorknob, unable to see through the tears in her eyes. She had to get in the house before she lost it completely.

The door swung open, and she shot through, closing it behind her and slumping down against it, her butt landing on the cold tile floor. Tears flowed down her face, and she sobbed, deep sobs that came from the marrow of her bones.

In her logical mind, she could appreciate the irony that she hadn't shed a single tear over someone she'd been thinking of marrying for years, but she couldn't stop the loud, painful wailing over the tall, straight man who didn't even live in a house.

# Chapter Nineteen

The next morning, Kelly woke late with swollen eyes made worse by the fact that it had been after five a.m. before she'd ever fallen asleep.

She called Tough first thing. Maybe it was wrong, but she'd give everything up for him. But his phone didn't even ring. There was no voice mail. She tried several more times before she absolutely had to head out.

She barely made it to work on time and had trouble concentrating, despite the large workload and her normal love of her job, anxiously awaiting the moment when she could leave.

By the time she met Mrs. Fitzsimmons to shop for her dress, the swelling around her eyes had gone down, although the dark shadows remained.

"I didn't think Preston upset you that much, honey," Mrs. Fitzsimmons said as they walked into the dress shop together.

Kelly sighed. "He didn't. I just have some other things on my mind."

"Were you worried about the speech? I didn't think it would be a problem." Her brows furrowed. "I feel bad about asking last minute. But someone from one of the media outlets we own is going to make some kind of a big announcement. There's going to be more people than we anticipated to begin with and also a big media presence. This is even better for you." Her kind eyes searched Kelly's face. "Is that okay?"

Kelly patted her hand. "That's great. And you were right about the speech. I had it done early last evening, and I'm not nervous or upset about it. The more people who can hear about our charity work, the better. No. It's nothing to do with you."

Mrs. Fitzsimmons looked worried, and Kelly felt a little bad about not sharing something she normally would have, but how does one explain that one doesn't believe in love but had just had her heart broken?

That's really what it felt like. Her chest hurt. Actual pain. It also felt empty at the same time, if that were even possible. And with every breath she took, she wanted to run to Tough. He'd take her. He'd love her. He said so.

But so had so many countless couples who had gone on to brutally split their families in two, separating because they'd *fallen out of love*.

She couldn't do it.

They found a perfect dress—deep cobalt blue, fitted to mid-thigh where it flared out and fell below her knees. It brought out her eyes and would look amazing with her string of pearls and dangly pearl earrings.

Mrs. Fitzsimmons had still not been convinced that she was okay by the time they parted with barely enough time for Kelly to get ready.

Barely. But she made it, pulling up to the valet parking with five minutes to spare.

She didn't normally wear extremely high heels for her job, and she stumbled for a step as she gave her keys to the valet. Righting herself, she remembered the night before when her world tilted crazily, but Tough had been there to steady her. Trying to shake the oddly bereft feeling off, she tucked her clutch close and strode with as much confidence as she could project into the brightly lit and tastefully decorated Mansion Heights.

Chatting briefly with a few people who stopped her, she made her way to the table she'd sat at for years with Cassidy and Mrs. Fitzsimmons. Normally Harris skipped the gala. She wasn't big on crowds, and although she helped with Helping Hearts, her own heart was with the library and her current project of raising funds for a children's library at the hospital. Kelly was a little surprised to see her sitting beside Cassidy, chatting with her and Torque.

Mrs. Fitzsimmons hadn't made it yet, but sometimes she was fashionably late.

Kelly didn't wonder about it too much. She had to make it through the evening. That's all. Maybe she would call in sick tomorrow. She never did, couldn't remember the last time she'd missed work, but she was definitely heartsick. Something in her wanted to crawl into a hole and die. There was another part of her that wanted to drive out to the warehouse she shared with Tough—used to share with Tough—and see if he really did move out. All his stuff...was it really gone? She could hardly believe it.

Her eyes widened as the crowd parted and she caught a brief glimpse of someone who looked an awful lot like Tough near the stage. People milled around, and she couldn't see anymore. She craned her neck, moving to the right. Her shoulder hit something hard, and she turned in time to see she'd maneuvered right into a waiter carrying a tray of champagne. It fell to the floor with a crash and shattering of glass.

"Oh, my goodness! I'm so sorry." She fell to her knees and began picking up pieces of broken glass.

"No, miss. I've got it, miss. Oh, please let me, miss." The waiter pushed her aside, and she stood, knowing her cheeks were bright red.

How stupid. Tough would not be here. He'd never been to one of these before. Ever. She obviously was completely crazy. And clumsy too.

Backing away, she put her head down, so she wouldn't see any apparitions that looked like Tough, and walked straight to her table. No more running into waiters, for goodness' sake.

She didn't get a chance to say anything to Harris because she realized as she arrived at the table that Bonita was sitting by Mrs. Fitzsimmons's empty chair. Kelly took a deep breath, slapped a smile on her face, and greeted the woman who had stolen her fiancé. Kelly shoved that thought aside. She couldn't steal what Kelly had never had.

The food was probably delicious. Kelly didn't know because she couldn't taste the small amount she managed to force down her throat.

Hopefully she carried her end of the conversation around the table of eight. She wasn't really present for it but hoped that habit kept her responses correct and timely.

Everything had to go smoothly now. She wouldn't embarrass her friends or the mother who raised her. She would do her part to raise money for the children who needed it. Later, when she was home alone, she could fall apart. Right now, she had to hold it together.

There were awards, but Kelly couldn't tell who won or what the awards were for. She clapped when everyone around her clapped. After the second award, she turned, watching with everyone else as the awardee walked up the steps. A man caught her eye. Dark hair, dark eyes. Brooding. Staring at her. He looked so much like Tough, it snapped her out of her daze. But then the people at the tables between them shifted, and she lost sight of him.

When the next awardee walked up, she was ready. Same man. Wearing a tux. The snowy white shirt contrasting with his dark tan. Her heart beat in her throat. She'd bet money it was Tough, except...what would he be doing here? She lost sight of him again.

"Hey, Kelly. They just announced you." Cassidy reached over Torque and tapped Kelly's shoulder.

Kelly blinked. Everyone was clapping, looking at her, and smiling. Her speech. She fumbled for her purse where her notes were, standing at the same time. Her purse slipped out of her frozen fingers, spilling onto the floor. Notecards fluttered all over the floor.

She swallowed and bent, grabbing her cards, which would be useless unless she took the time to reorder them. She didn't.

Walking to the stairs, she ascended to the platform. Her knees shook, and she clasped her hands together so they wouldn't do the same. Her stomach felt like she'd just ingested poison. Once she started speaking, she'd be fine. She always was.

But as she stood at the podium and opened her mouth to tell the joke she had planned as an icebreaker, her eyes drifted to the right side of the room where the man who looked like Tough had been sitting. He was still there. And he still looked exactly like Tough. She couldn't help doing a double take. It *was* Tough. Most definitely. But what was he doing here? Why? How?

Her mouth opened, and words came out, but she had no idea of what she was saying, if it made sense, or even if it was in English. Not a clue. She rambled on for what felt like a very long time, until she finally finished and almost ran off the stage. Planning to go straight out the door, she stopped at the table to retrieve her purse.

Harris grabbed her arm. "No. You can't leave. Sit. The same people who are sponsoring this gala own the syndicated rights to Dr. T's column! They're going to tell us who Dr. T is!"

Huh? Kelly looked at Harris who was beet red and bouncing in her seat but holding so tightly to Kelly's arm that she couldn't pull away without causing a scene.

She dropped down in her chair, setting her clutch on the table, hoping it didn't take long. She could hardly wait to get home and hide under her covers. Forget calling in sick tomorrow. She was taking the rest of the week off.

Determined to suffer through, she tried to turn the corners of her mouth up as she looked toward the stage.

Tough stood at the podium. People were clapping. Even with his tan, she could tell his face was flushed. Sweat shone on his forehead. He used one hand to pull at the black tie around his neck. The cords in his neck popped out, dark against the white of his shirt. He looked just as amazing in this tux as he had in the one at Cassidy's wedding.

Kelly realized the video cameras at the bottom of the stage were news crews. And a lot of them. They must have moved in as she was stumbling to her seat. Bright lights shone on the stage as the audience seemed to hold its breath in anticipation. What was going on? Was Tough announcing Dr. T? But why? Because Dr. T's column had started out as a mechanic's column? Nothing else made sense.

Tough stood at the podium. The audience had been quiet for a while. But his tongue hung in his mouth. He'd spent so much of the last month or so working hard to get it to move, for Kelly's sake. Heck, no. Who was he kidding? For his sake. So he could talk to her. He'd forced that little member to move to his command, and he'd held actual conversations with the most wonderful person he'd ever known. Right up through last night.

Fire exploded in his stomach at the thought of kissing Kelly. It had been so far beyond anything he'd ever experienced. He'd wanted to stay, to just hold her and kiss her all night. That same fire, though, threatened to consume him because he hadn't thought they could be together. He'd lost everything.

Maybe he could have found a place to move his garage which was closer to Brickly Springs. But part of him, for self-preservation, had known that he needed to leave. Otherwise he'd spend the rest of his life trying to convince her to be with him, to love him back, despite the fact that he had nothing.

Ah, yeah. There was the problem. He knew he didn't really deserve her love anyway. His dad had left, no love there. His mother had died. And it was so very easy to overlook the kid that never talked.

The silence had continued long enough to be awkward. The audience moved and rustled, getting restless.

Tough's eyes, which had been staring at the back of the room, over everyone's head, skimmed across the room until they met Kelly's. He wasn't going to give her the chance to ruin her life by being with him, but maybe, maybe if she were willing to take a chance on him, he wouldn't say no.

His lip twitched. Her mouth smiled in return. The most beautiful thing he'd ever seen was Kelly smiling at him.

He opened his mouth. "Good evening, y'all."

"Good evening," everyone said back.

"I have an announcement." No point in beating around the bush.

There was some tittering.

"You probably don't know who I am." Silence. He met Kelly's eyes again. She knew him. Better than anyone. He pulled from her strength. "I'm a mechanic. I also do body work. I had a shop, Tough Bodywork, midtown, but I've just moved it about an hour away to Berryville." He took a breath. His hands were still shaking so bad, he didn't even bother trying to reach into his jacket and pull out the notecard that he'd scratched down some notes on. There wasn't that much to say anyway, although his syndicated sponsors wanted him to talk about his history and how he got where he was.

The audience shifted. His knees shook. His gaze went back to Kelly, and he plunged in again. "Back when I first started out, I was trying to build clientele, and I came up with this idea to start an advice column for people who had questions about their cars. Made sense. I called it Tough Talk. It was moderately successful. But what I found was that men would ask me about their cars then ask me about their relationships too. Or maybe just complain about their relationships."

The audience tittered, and he loosened up some. At least his legs didn't feel like they were going to collapse. He set his feet and gripped the podium with both hands.

"I never had a relationship myself. The only girl I'd ever wanted turned me down the one time I got up the courage to ask her." He paused and gave a wry grin while a few members of the audience chuckled. "I did a lot of watching, and I took a few stabs at answering the guys' questions. To my shock, my suggestions seemed to work, because they would come back or write back thanking me." He shrugged. The audience laughed.

"Somehow, over the years, the column got shortened to T, and someone started calling me Dr. T. I never claimed to be a doctor, but it was kind of funny to me, because I am a car doctor, so I let it stick."

He swallowed, wishing he had some water to wet his dry throat. He wasn't used to talking this much, even without being in front of a crowd. But he needed to do this. "I never thought the column would see this much success. I know there are people who would say I'm doing harm, because I'm giving out advice and I don't have a degree. Well, I say to those people, they've never hung out in a garage shop before. I see stuff every day." He waved his hand. How to describe the pain that walked through his door every single day. Sure, he did oil changes, but people often showed up at his door when they'd just had something horrible—a car accident—happen to them.

He continued slowly. "People suffering, making mistakes. I see how they act when they're angry, when they're desperate. I've watched people handle their problems with grace and class, and I've watched people fall apart in front of me. I've been attacked. More than once.

Maybe watching and listening, thinking and learning doesn't make me a professional anything, but when I add a dose of everyday common sense and let the psychobabble out, people seem to listen, to respond, and I've seen them change their lives for the better."

It was true. People responded to straight talk. Tough talk.

"I guess, now that you've seen me, you might think I shouldn't be here, shouldn't have a column, shouldn't have the privilege of having people come to me for advice." He snorted and gripped the podium tighter. "I don't have all the answers. I have problems of my own that I can't solve." Man, he was really off script now. "I have someone sitting in here this evening, who deserves to feel hurt and betrayed because I hid something important from her."

He looked directly at the news crews. "That's the unveiling. Dr. T, mechanic advice columnist, is me, Tough Baxter." He stared for a last few seconds before he rapped his knuckles on the podium, turned, and walked off the stage.

In the back, someone began clapping. He had started to descend the steps, but he looked up to see his brother, Torque, standing with Cassidy. Their whole table stood up, clapping. Except...

Soon the entire audience was on its feet.

But his eyes were on Kelly. She stood beside Cassidy, her back to him, her arms around...Preston. She was hugging Preston like she'd never let him go.

While Tough watched, Kelly grabbed her purse, Preston grabbed her hand, and they hurried out the back door. Together.

He was asked to go back up and answer questions, but he declined, slipping out a side door. His tongue had worked, and he had faced the crowd of people, but he had reached his limit, and he needed to go somewhere quiet and nurse his broken heart.

# Chapter Twenty

Kelly walked into the activity center. Kids ran around playing freeze tag on the unfinished gym floor. Her eyes searched for Jasmine. There. Smiling and chasing another girl. Kelly's heart warmed. Maybe Jasmine would be okay.

A teenaged girl sat on a low chair at a little table surrounded by toddlers who all had a big chunk of playdough. On the other side, middle school kids sat at tables with their books spread out in front of them and at the kitchenette. Mr. Sigel stood in front of the coffee maker.

Wait, what? Mr. Sigel?

Kelly hurried over. She had wondered what Al and Mr. Sigel and the other half-dozen or so less-regular retirees would do without being able to hang out at Tough's garage. She didn't think they'd move with him. She grinned. Apparently, they were going to hang out here.

Before she reached him, her phone buzzed, and she dug it out. A text from her banker.

> I have a donor for you. Can you come to the
> bank and sign papers today?

Her pulse quickened. She texted back quickly.

I'll be there soon.

If she hurried, she could make it before five.

"Mr. Sigel." She held her arms out, and he wrapped her in a warm embrace, smelling slightly of bengay and coffee. She missed the grease and exhaust smell that had always been a part of him, too, but shoved that thought aside.

"Kelly. Good to see you. Want coffee?" he asked in his grizzled voice.

"No thanks. I'm heading home for the day."

"Al already left. Can't stand me beating him at checkers." Mr. Sigel winked.

Kelly looked over at the checkerboard, which sat on its barrel among the desks. Tough had moved it over without asking, which was fine with her. It was his way of taking care of Mr. Sigel and Al, she supposed.

"I see."

Mr. Sigel touched her arm with a gnarled finger. "The old folks around are really going to miss Tough."

"I know," Kelly said. "But you can let everyone know that they are always welcome to come here and hang out."

"You're not going to fix our cars for free, are you?"

"No, of course not." Kelly hesitated. Had Tough fixed everyone's car for free? "What do you mean, free? Tough never charged anyone?"

"Just senior citizens. He didn't advertise or anything, but we all knew he wouldn't charge us for any work we got done in his shop. He didn't charge anything, not even parts."

No wonder there were always so many elderly people. She'd wondered about that. "I see." Tough, of course, had never let on, never said a thing, and that's the issue she most had trouble getting over. Just like Preston, who hid his longtime girlfriend for over a decade, Tough had hid not only the fact that he apparently did work for free for anyone who was retired, and who knew who else, but that he also had a very famous, very popular, very profitable advice column. That she'd written in to! Her temple throbbed every time she thought of it.

It wasn't exactly fair to compare him to Preston. She knew that.

Mr. Sigel leaned in closer and lowered his voice, like he was delivering state secrets. "I think he even did free work for poor people too. He's nice but not a very good businessman. You can't give away stuff for free and make money." He patted her arm. "He's a good fellow, though. I thought maybe you'd...well, he just seemed to come out of his shell, so to speak, when you showed up. I thought you might see the real Tough, you know? People only see what they want to, and no one ever bothered to look at him before."

Kelly pressed her lips together. She didn't want to be served a guilt trip on top of everything else, but Mr. Sigel was right. She saw the real Tough, and she really shouldn't have been surprised about the free work he did. The advice column, though? No way. She should not have seen that.

That had shocked her clear to her toes and back.

"Well, I have to run to the bank before it closes, so I'm heading out."

"Keep the old folks in mind if you find another good, cheap mechanic." Mr. Sigel picked his coffee up and shuffled over to the checkerboard.

Kelly drove to the bank, deliberately trying not to think about Tough or the depths that she hadn't even realized he had. Had she truly been blind? And did it matter?

Her phone rang. She pressed the button to use the car's speaker. "Hello?"

"Hey," Cassidy said. "How's Mrs. Fitzsimmons?"

"She's doing much better." Poor Preston had been so overwrought when he'd found out during the charity gala that his mother had driven herself to the ER with chest pain that he'd forgotten all about Bonita. Maybe because he was so used to reaching for Kelly in public, out of habit, but whatever, he'd grabbed Kelly in a hug before snatching her hand and running out. Kelly had felt bad for him, and of course, she'd been concerned about Mrs. Fitzsimmons, too. "It was a bad case of heartburn. But I'm glad she got it checked out."

"Too bad she missed the gala," Cassidy said.

"Yeah. It's the first one she'd missed in twenty years." Kelly felt bad that she'd never even noticed. She'd been so wrapped up in Tough.

Crying erupted in the background. Cassidy said, "I have to run, but

I wanted you to know that Torque said Turbo ran over Tough's phone when they were moving his stuff out of the garage."

"On purpose?"

"It was Turbo, so that's a legitimate question," Cassidy said with a laugh. "But, no, Turbo insists he didn't mean to. Anyway, I wasn't sure if maybe you might have been trying to get a hold of him..." Her voice trailed off.

Kelly didn't answer. That made sense. Why Tough wasn't taking her calls. Why they didn't even go to voice mail. A little blossom of hope stirred in her chest.

More crying. "I have to go." Cassidy hung up.

Kelly tapped the steering wheel. Maybe because Tough lost his mother, maybe because he was poor growing up, but somehow, he'd gotten it in his head that he wasn't good enough for her. Of all their problems, that one was ridiculous. But it was so real to him.

Could the problems that she felt were so huge between them be the same? Ridiculous? Did she have to be in Brickly Springs? Weren't there kids that could use her help in Berryville, too? Why couldn't she be with Tough in Berryville and find people who needed her there?

Still contemplating those questions, she walked into the bank and greeted Tina, her banker. Tina led her to her office. Kelly sat at Tina's desk in front of a stack of papers.

"My mother had a car accident. She's fine, but it's been a crazy day. I would have gotten a hold of you sooner..." Tina bustled around her desk, grabbing a pen. Her normally neat hair flew around her head, and her shirt was partially untucked in the back. She was also missing an earring.

Tina's phone rang. She threw a couple more papers on the pile in front of Kelly.

"Here, look these over. I need to answer this." She turned toward the window and answered in her professional banking voice.

Kelly picked up the pen and papers. She'd done this before, and usually it was very straightforward. She perused the papers, noting the exceptional amount, donated weekly and deposited directly into her checking account, which caused her chest to buzz. She would have enough to pay the rent for the activity center every month!

She also noted that the donor desired to remain anonymous. But stuck in the middle of the pile were papers that were unfamiliar. The donor papers, apparently, that Tina, in her haste, had accidentally added to her stack. Before she could shove the papers aside, her eyes caught on a name. A familiar, beloved name. Tough Baxter.

She pushed away from the table and walked out.

# Chapter Twenty-One

Tough sat on a five-gallon oil bucket outside his new shop. Darkness had fallen hours ago, coming early as it did this time of year. He fingered the cigarette in his hand, flipping it around, back and forth, through his fingers. He didn't need it anymore. Heck, anyone who could stand up in front of hundreds of people and talk as long as he had couldn't fault their tongue for anything.

Shifting, he pulled the lighter out of his pocket, snapped it open, and clicked. The flame burst out, bright and hot, before settling down to a steady glow. Wasn't that like love? Like relationships, where they burned hot and strong for the first while, before settling down into a steady and predictable routine. Wasn't that the natural order of things? He couldn't believe Kelly was right that passionate love didn't matter because it didn't last.

His lighter sputtered and went out.

He almost laughed. There was an answer. According to his lighter, Kelly was right.

But people, couples, didn't run out of energy. Not unless they chose to, right? What if he chose to never give up on his relationship and he was with someone who chose the same thing? Never give up. No matter what. He wouldn't walk away. He wouldn't leave. He wouldn't quit loving Kelly, even if that love didn't look the same ten years from now as it did today.

He shoved the empty lighter back in his pocket and tossed the cigarette out into the street. None of it mattered, and he was wasting his time trying to figure it out. Even if Kelly believed in love, in his love, he'd betrayed her by hiding his column, answering her anonymously, and he couldn't blame her for finding him easy to walk away from.

He couldn't forget, either, that loving someone was painful, too. He'd loved his mother and lost her. He'd never really recovered from it. Maybe that was the real reason that he hadn't pursued Kelly harder but had walked away so easily. Maybe it was really fear that clutched his heart and made him think he wasn't good enough.

He leaned back on the bucket, putting his hands behind his head and looking up at the stars. At least here, in Berryville, which was a smaller town, the stars were brighter. That was one good thing. Still, he hadn't found his niche yet, and he was used to the hustle of a full shop and tons of work, not to mention he missed the old guys who hung out in his shop. He closed his eyes, knowing he wasn't fooling himself. He missed Kelly.

The hum of a motor cut through his thoughts, and he opened his eyes to headlights swinging around the corner. A car, a Prius, very similar to Kelly's, pulled into the curb. It couldn't be Kelly, but his heart leaped from its comatose position in his chest and jumped up and down. Couldn't kill hope.

The headlights shut off, and he saw the blond head through the windshield. His bucket slammed down on the pavement, but he waited for her door to open and for her to step out before he stood.

She closed her car door and folded her hands over her chest.

Not a good sign. He shoved his hands in his pockets and leaned a shoulder back against the building.

"You told me." She tapped her foot on the pavement.

He wanted to just stand there, since he had no idea what she was talking about, but he forced his mouth to move. "What?"

"In your column. The answer to my question. You told me that you were hiding things."

A cool breeze blew, and Kelly shivered, wrapping her arms around herself. Tough wanted to go wrap his arms around her and give her his heat.

"I deceived you. I'm sorry." Apologizing wasn't hard, because he meant it.

"Preston deceived me too." She tilted her head. "He's had a girlfriend since we were in ninth grade."

Tough's chest constricted at the pain in her voice. But his heart also hurt because she seemed to be lumping him in the same group as Preston.

Maybe because of the dark, maybe because he'd been practicing, maybe because he needed her to see, but the words somehow tumbled off his tongue. "There's never been anyone for me but you."

"You're not like Preston." She continued in a softer tone, "That's not the only secret."

He looked back up at the stars, knowing she was right and having no defense.

She ticked them off on her finger. "The column. Giving free service and repairs from your garage. Moving out of your side of the garage so I didn't have to."

His head snapped up, and she nodded fiercely. "Oh, yeah. I know about that. Mr. Millard came in, and we had an interesting conversation. Then there are the papers at the bank with your name on them. The ones I wasn't supposed to see that named you as the donor of enough money to pay my rent every month. Tell me, Tough." Her foot tapped staccato bursts on the pavement. "Is that money from your column?"

"Yeah," he answered, closing his eyes.

Beats of silence passed, broken only by distant rumbling of a Cummins motor on the interstate and the tapping of Kelly's foot.

"Aren't you going to say anything?" she asked, her voice hinting at pain and anger.

He jerked his shoulders off the wall and sauntered over, getting right in her face but not touching, his breath coming in short pants, the veins in his neck feeling ready to burst. "You weren't mine. You were never mine. You wore Preston's ring. I can't bare my heart and soul to you when you've got another man's ring on your finger."

She held her hands up, all her fingers bare. "Preston's out of the picture. I told you when it happened. Are there more secrets?"

The lack of a ring was a good sign; his heart wanted to sing. But she wanted his secrets. He fisted his hands in his pockets and forced himself to meet her eyes, the words heavy and slow at first, but at least they came out. "Every day, every hour, I stop myself from begging you to take a chance on me. That's what's in here." He hit his chest. "I lie awake at night trying to figure out how I can convince you that what I feel for you isn't some passing fancy that's going to be gone in a year or fifty. At the same time, I fight myself constantly because I'm not good enough for you and I don't deserve you and I've never given a flip about money, but I was tempted to move here and keep the money from my column and start charging everyone who walks into my shop full rate so I have the cash to buy a house and provide the life you deserve and I might have a snowball's chance in hell of being able to give you a fraction of what Preston could."

His nose was millimeters from hers, but he had his hands shoved deep in his pockets so he wasn't tempted to grab her and shake her or, more likely, kiss her.

"Anything else?" she asked in a more subdued tone.

He backed off, just a hair, and said softly, "I tell myself not to be afraid just because the only other woman I've ever loved—my mother—died. Because sometimes love hurts."

She blinked and bit her lip. "Is that it?"

"I'm not hiding another blasted thing."

Her head tilted, and a little smile lifted the corner of her mouth. "Do you want to know what I've been hiding?"

The question, spoken softly, drained some of his righteous anger. He searched her face in the dim light, hoping for a clue as to whether it was something he really wanted to know. He already felt like he'd gone through open heart surgery. But he didn't have a chance to think before his mouth moved. "What?"

"I know you'll love me to the end of time, because that's the kind of man you are." His breath caught. "The problem is I don't know what kind of woman I am."

"Isn't that for me to take a chance on?" he asked, trying not to allow the hope in his heart to blossom.

"Don't you see? The problem isn't are you good enough for me. The problem is whether I'm good enough for you." Her voice raised, and her hands flew up in the air. "All those things you were 'hiding'? They were all for my good. You would never do anything to hurt me, and I know it. But me..." She hung her head. "I know I'm not good enough for you. Not even close."

"Do I get any say in this?" He used a finger to brush back a stray hair from her face before allowing it to track down her cheek.

Her hand came up and twined her fingers with his.

"I want to protect you from the wrong choice," she whispered, closing her eyes.

"Then you'd better stick pretty close. If you marry me, that might be close enough."

"If you're willing to settle for me..."

"I'm not settling," he interrupted. He couldn't stand hearing her say that. "I haven't had anyone drop my column. I might keep making money at it. I could keep the money and buy us a house..."

She put her fingers over his mouth. "Shh. I don't mind any of that. Everything I've done, all the work for kids and charity, has never been about needing money for material things. It's always been about trying to provide the family that I didn't have."

That hurt. Thinking of little Kelly so many years ago, dirty and sad, just wanting someone to love her. His heart cracked a little. If it was the last thing he did, he would be there for her, be the family she never had, be the rock she could depend on. If only she would accept and believe. "I'm not leaving you, Kelly."

"I know." She held his face in her hands. He turned his head slightly to kiss her fingers. "I love you, Tough."

His heart almost exploded with happiness, and a thrill jolted down his body. He smiled. "I need to hear that about thirty times a day for the rest of my life." He bent down and kissed her.

A lot of time later, he sat on the bucket, Kelly snuggled in his lap. She needed to go home. He needed to get to bed.

"Oh, I forgot," Kelly murmured sleepily.

"What?" Tough asked absently, stroking her hair.

"Cassidy said that the city council was not going to issue the new owner of the building a permit for his strip club, since there was a juvenile facility in the same building." She tapped his chest. "You gave up your garage for me, but you can have it back. Mr. Millard said the buyer cancelled the closing. He offered it to us."

"That's good…if he'll rent it."

Kelly laughed. "Okay. So maybe I had another small secret. But it's only because you kissed me and made me forget everything I ever knew."

"You and me both." Tough grinned.

"Whatever I said at the charity gala must have been convincing because I've had a ton of donations come in for the activity center. Not enough to cover the purchase price, but enough to make a big enough down payment on the building so our payment would be about the same as rent."

"And my column can pay that."

"Yep," she said and snuggled closer, her hand splayed over his chest, like she was holding his heart. Which she was. "I don't know what you'll do with this building, though."

"I don't know either." But one thing he did know. "It'll work out." He leaned down and kissed her again.

TURBO BAXTER STOOD outside the pole building, his head leaned back against the cold metal, his eyes squeezed shut. He'd shove his hands in his pockets, except he was wearing a monkey suit and there were no pockets.

The teachers in school had been right. He was stupid.

Man, he'd had the biggest crush on Harris Winstead, since elementary school, and he'd just wanted her to notice him. But like all the other things he'd done over the years to impress her or to get her attention, tonight's fiasco had made it look like he hated her and wanted to embarrass her.

He'd get over it. His natural optimism always rose to the top. But she might not.

Just once, he'd like to be able to have a conversation with her. But he couldn't seem to stop his hyper personality and over-active brain from working overtime and making everything he tried, over-the-top and annoying, rather than the charming he'd intended.

He'd really screwed up tonight.

Of course her speech comparing him to Indiana Jones's pet monkey had been pretty funny.

Kelly and Tough had looked happy together. They'd laughed. And Kelly had barely given him the hairy eyeball after he'd spilt the punch. On Harris.

She didn't know what he'd done to her dress.

He was fooling himself anyway. Harris was a librarian. She loved books and reading and studying. Sitting still. Quietness. All things he admired about her. Probably because they were all things that he couldn't do. All of them.

But that was a secret. Harris could never find out.

Join Jessie's list and be the first to know about new releases and sales on her books!

Read Still with You, the next book in the Baxter Boys series where Turbo meets his match in quiet librarian Harris. Will the secret he's keeping destroy the trust they've built between them? Keep reading for a sneak peek now.

# Sneak Peek of Still With You

Harris Winsted opened the heavy library door, shifted the massive bulk of papers and books in her arms, and stepped out into the brisk evening air. It had cost her a modest fortune, which was no insignificant thing on her small-town librarian's salary, but she had printed off the copyright-allotted thirty copies of the production of *Annie* the community players were doing to raise money for a children's library at the new pediatric cancer hospital.

Two opposing pangs pushed through her chest. Excitement and fear. Being able to sponsor a library for kids in the hospital was a dream come true for her. After all, she knew exactly how it felt to be cooped up for months on end having read everything in sight, including every word on the shampoo bottles, at least five times. But she'd never directed a play before in her life. At least she wasn't acting in it. Getting up in front of people was a phobia she'd never conquered.

After juggling her keys and locking the door, she started down the small flight of steps that led to the sidewalk. A man's shout broke the stillness of the early fall air. A child's higher-pitched yell followed, then what sounded like a war-hoot from an elderly man. Harris smiled. It sounded like a family was having fun down the side alley that ran along the library. The next best thing to a family reading together was a family playing together.

She shoved down the tiny thread of longing that surged in her chest. The cancer treatments she'd had as a child had wiped any hope of having her own children from her life. She was too studious and serious to have children of her own anyway.

The stomping of footsteps declared they were now running. It almost sounded like the whirl of a bike tire back there too.

Her high heel clicked on the cement as she stepped off the last step onto the sidewalk. The laughing and shouting had gotten closer. She shifted the heavy stack of papers, wishing that the hole punch hadn't chosen today to get stuck in the closed position. No amount of grunting, pushing, or under-her-breath—because it was a library after all—swearing had managed to get it to work. So her precious, expensive copies of *Annie* lay stacked, alternated by long and short edge, on top of the pile of books she was delivering to the assisted care facility on her way home.

The shouts got louder as a blur from her left made her turn her head. Barely able to see over the top of her pile of books and precious papers, she blinked. Then squinted. It wasn't every day one saw a wheelchair rounding the corner on two wheels. She looked just as the man in it was smiling so hard his teeth popped out. They fell to the cement as the much younger man pushing it cornered sharply, the chair almost horizontal to the ground. The man's biceps bulged. A helmeted boy on rollerblades, legs churning, screamed, "I'm going to win! You can't beat me!" as his right skate hit the dentures. His hands windmilled, florescent green sleeves a blur as his shouted challenge turned to a startled yelp. The dentures skidded to the side where one of the younger man's scuffed brown boots nicked them, throwing him off balance. Harris's eyebrows flew up to her hairline. Her brain shouted at her feet to pedal backward, but in the heels, they were slow to respond.

The boy grabbed the wheelchair handle to keep from falling. Able to right the chair despite the added pressure, the man pushing the chair overcompensated, and he took two wild, uncoordinated steps before his body crashed into Harris.

Papers and books flew everywhere.

As she flew downward toward the ground, she couldn't help but try to search her memory...were the pages numbered?

Fully expecting to crack her head on the cement steps, Harris was surprised to land with a thump on the solid chest of the pusher.

She had no idea how he'd managed to reverse their positions before they hit the ground, but she was grateful, except...

The man's ball cap had gone askew, and his curling brown hair and laughing brown eyes were now visible. Turbo Baxter.

Harris felt her cheeks heat and knew her entire face would be as red as her hair. All seven million of her freckles would be camouflaged under that brighter color. Unfortunately, her complexion looked even worse as fire-engine red than it did as the regular porcelain white splotched with enough freckles to cover the north side of the Empire State Building. Twice.

"I should have known when I heard that unholy screeching that you had something to do with it," she said to the man under her. She blew a hair out of her eyes and tried to figure out how she was going to get off him since she'd foolishly decided to wear a pencil skirt and skyscraper heels today.

She couldn't look at Turbo again. With amusement crinkling his eyes, and with his sharp Roman nose and angled jaw, the man was sinfully handsome—cover model material for the romance novels she loved to read at night—but he had the maturity level of a two-year-old. She wouldn't be horizontal with her papers scattered to the four winds if he had the sense God gave a squirrel.

He grunted under her. "I should have known that you'd manage to turn a simple footrace into an obstacle course." His biceps flexed, stretching the sleeves of his t-shirt as he shifted, pushing her off and up, away from the intriguing scent of raw masculinity overlaid with just a hint of fun. A scent she remembered clearly from last summer's wedding when she had the misfortune to be in the same bridal party as Turbo. She had been lucky enough to have not seen him since.

"I'm sorry my presence on the sidewalk confused you." She brushed her skirt off and looked at the boy, who didn't seem to be bleeding, then at the old man in the wheelchair who had somehow gotten his dentures off the ground and was using his shirt to wipe them off. He popped them into his mouth before holding out his hand in a somehow gallant gesture.

"That's Mr. Pollack. But everyone calls him Pap," Turbo said from above her shoulder. "Pap, this is the fussy librarian, Ms. Winsted." Turbo ducked down and started picking up papers.

Harris cringed at his calloused unconcern for her precious play copies and narrowed her eyes, but she didn't get a chance to say anything before Pap spoke. "I'm so sorry Turbo ran into you. Typically, he runs away from women."

"I think you have that backward," Harris muttered as she shook his hand.

"DeShaun, help Turbo gather the nice lady's papers up, please," the elderly man said, waving a gnarled hand around. Her papers littered the ground like a blanket. At least it wasn't windy.

"I wouldn't say 'nice,'" Turbo mumbled under his breath. "Prissy, maybe."

"I can hear you," Harris spat out at him as she bent and picked up several papers. They weren't numbered. Just her luck.

"I'm sorry."

Her hand, holding a fistful of papers, stilled. She turned slowly. Turbo Baxter had just apologized. His face actually oozed sincerity.

"I shouldn't have gotten so upset about you deliberately stepping right in front of us, on purpose. Then you shoved me down and fell on top of me, and you're not exactly a lightweight." Turbo lifted his hat and shoved a hand through his longish curls. His lip twitched, ruining the earnestness of his apology as if his words already hadn't.

Harris's lips compressed together. That's exactly what Turbo had done at the wedding last year when she'd been stuck in the bridal party with him, and it's exactly what he'd done in high school. Not that she'd spent much time with him then, either. Although her most unforgettable high school memory had to be when she'd been voted most studious and he'd been voted class clown. They had to get their picture taken together. The photographer thought it would be funny to snap a pic of Harris reading a book with Turbo on a chair behind her pretending to be about to pour red paint over her head. Apparently, among his other numerous faults, Turbo didn't know what pretending meant, since he dumped the entire one-gallon can of fire-engine red paint on her. It made for a great picture, she supposed. But he ruined her dogeared version of *Anne of Green Gables*, which she had lovingly chosen from her numerous, beloved favorites to be the book in the photo. Then he spent the rest of the year making fun of her that he'd actually found something that was redder than her hair.

That might have been ten years ago, and she might have spent the last decade avoiding him, despite living in the same small town.

Keeping her back to him, she continued to pick her papers up. She'd learned in high school that the best way to deal with Turbo was to ignore him.

"Hey." He grabbed her elbow. "You're actually bleeding here. And I really am sorry."

She yanked her arm away and continued to pick up papers. The little boy chattered, handing his papers to the old man who tapped the piles against his leg and straightened them out a little before stacking them on his knees.

Harris's chest tightened. Hopefully she'd be able to put these scripts back together. She moved away from Turbo. He was probably just going to tell her he was joking, or she'd look up and he'd squirt ketchup on her or something equally annoying. Although her elbow did hurt. Like a brush burn. She'd look at it later.

Turbo appeared in her peripheral vision, knees bent, picking up papers and shuffling them together haphazardly. She turned from him and moved away before she said something really nasty.

He moved with her. "I'm serious. I didn't mean to run into you."

She didn't look at him. "Okay. So you're admitting it was your fault."

"And I'm apologizing. The nice thing is to say 'hey, it's okay.'"

"Well, it's really not okay. I just paid a fortune to buy the copyright to thirty scripts and print them off, and now they're all mixed up and practically ruined."

"I wish I could fix it. I really am sorry."

"Stop saying you're sorry!" She brushed her hair back over her shoulder. Her gaze fixed on a shiny, bright red drop on the paper she'd been about to pick up. Looked like blood. Great.

"I don't know how else to get you to believe me." He picked up the paper with the blood, looking at her. His nearness was distracting, and she went back to swiping papers from the sidewalk in order to keep from meeting his gaze.

The little boy had gathered all her books and straightened up after stacking them in a pile on the library steps.

She scooted away from Turbo, holding tight to her irritation. "If you're really sorry, you can help me arrange these papers in order and put them all back together." It would take hours. All night possibly. And she had wanted to hand out the scripts tomorrow evening at the first rehearsal. She held tight to a fistful of papers and stopped long enough to see Turbo's reaction.

He sighed and looked down at the papers. "Aren't they numbered?"

"No." She set her jaw against his crestfallen look.

His Adam's apple bobbed, and a muscle twitched in his jaw. "Oh." He turned away, bending over and grabbing the last few papers off the sidewalk. He shuffled them into a pile, reached down, and took the papers Pap handed him, awkwardly smoothing them altogether. "Here."

"You're not helping?" She didn't really want him to; he'd find a way to set her house on fire or defrost all the food in her freezer or paint her car pink or...something. After all, it was Turbo. But it was his fault that she had all the scattered papers to begin with. Although...

She looked at Pap, sitting in his chair while the little boy showed him something on his phone. Really, she needed to give Turbo points for hanging out with an elderly man and a young kid. It was Friday evening. He could be at a bar, trying to find a date for the night.

"No. I..." Turbo glanced at the man and boy. "I have plans for this evening."

Pap looked up from his chair. "Humph. Your only plans for this evening involved taking me back to prison, ahem, the nursing joint my daughters dumped me in then never visit, and flirting with Mrs. Silcrest while we play bingo. And trust me, Sally Silcrest will miss you, but your so-called 'stuffy librarian' is much better looking, not to mention about seventy years younger."

"Sally was going to bake me cookies," Turbo said. He shifted and shoved a hand in his front pocket. "Nothing's better than Sally's fresh-baked chocolate chips."

"Of course, Mr. Baxter." It hurt more than she cared to admit that he'd rather spend the evening at the nursing home watching the elderly residents play bingo than have to be in her presence for a few hours. But he probably did liven up the old folks' home. Wherever Turbo was, people were laughing. "I wouldn't want you to miss cookies, bingo, and flirting with a 90-year-old. I'll organize my own papers."

Harris put her nose in the air to hide her hurt and turned, bending to pick up the stack of books. Blood dripped from her arm to the step.

"She's bleeding all over the place," Pap said.

"Wow. She definitely needs a couple band-aids." The little boy scrunched up his face. "That's nasty."

"You're right, DeShaun." Turbo reached into his back pocket and pulled out a blue rag. "Let me see that." He reached for her elbow.

She would bleed out before she let him touch her with that dirty rag. Whether he used it to wipe his hands after working on his truck or to wipe his nose, the rag looked well-worn. "No thank you." She tried not to sound stuck-up, but she wasn't going to risk contracting flesh-eating bacteria by being polite in this instance. "I'll be fine until I get home."

"But..." DeShaun said.

Turbo's hands paused midair, and she was pretty sure he was offended.

"I'll be fine. Really." She tried to speak in a kind tone but to still be very firm. That rag was not touching her arm. She forced more words out. "Thanks for helping me clean up my papers." Even if it had been his fault they were dropped in the first place.

Guilt squeezed her throat. She'd known the hole punch was on its last legs. She should have replaced it before it quit.

Her arm burned.

"I can carry those books for you," Turbo said in a low tone as she started to walk away. "You taking them to your car?"

"No. To Redbud Manor."

"That's where we're going," DeShaun sang out. "Come on, Pap.

We'll beat the slowpokes." He pushed the wheelchair down the sidewalk, gliding behind on his rollerblades.

Harris tightened her lips. If only she had known. She would have said she was going in the opposite direction, just to get away from Turbo. Too late. Although, if she had to walk in the same direction as him, she might as well let him carry the books. Not the papers.

She turned back around to see him watching her. Turbo with those brown eyes hooded under his ball cap. Probably his next prank was simmering in his brain, and she'd be on the receiving end. Well, he could still carry the books.

As soon as she looked at him, he stepped forward with his hands out, reaching for her books. Against her better judgment, she held them out, trying to separate them from the stack of papers under them. How could she not notice his hands which were strong and tanned with long fingers? Capable hands. Hands that knew how to work. Hands that could grip an old man's wheelchair and race down the street, making the fellow laugh while racing with a young boy who seemed to be having a great time. His fingers curled around her books, and a surprising bit of heat curled in her stomach.

One of the books started to slide, and they both reached for it. Their hands clashed together. Shockwaves rolled up her arm, intensifying the burning in her elbow. Her startled gaze flew to his. Close enough now that she could see his eyes under the curled brim of his cap, she watched as they widened as though mirroring her own.

She searched his face, noticed the tightening of his jaw, the small twitch of his lips, before feeling the shifting pile of books and grabbing for them. Turbo's hands reached out at the same time, and they collided again, only this time she lost her grip on everything, and it all fell down again. Papers and books back in a heaped-up mess on the sidewalk.

Sign up for Jessie's newsletter! Get a free book, access to exclusive bonus content, get fun and funny updates on her life on the farm and more!

# Read More Jessie!

Tap here to see all of Jessie's books!

# A Gift from Jessie

*View this code through your smart phone camera to be taken to a page where you can download a FREE ebook when you sign up to get updates from Jessie Gussman! Find out why people say, "Jessie's is the only newsletter I open and read" and "You make my day brighter. Love, love, love reading your newsletters. I don't know where you find time to write books. You are so busy living life. A true blessing." and "I know from now on that I can't be drinking my morning coffee while reading your newsletter – I laughed so hard I sprayed it out all over the table!"*

Claim your free book from Jessie!